REVENGE
OF THE NERD

REVENGE OF THE NERD

John McNamara

DELACORTE PRESS / NEW YORK

Library of Congress Cataloging in Publication Data
McNamara, John [date of birth].
    Revenge of the nerd.
    Summary: A ninth-grade genius with a reputation for
being a nerd wreaks revenge on his tormentors using his
latest science project, by which he can invade their
homes via their television screens.
    [1. High schools—Fiction. 2. Schools—Fiction]
I. Title.
PZ7.M478793Re 1984   [Fic]
ISBN 0-385-29348-8
Library of Congress Catalog Card Number: 84-4328

Published by
Delacorte Press
1 Dag Hammarskjold Plaza
New York, N.Y. 10017

This work is based on the television program *Revenge of the Nerd*, written by John McNamara and produced by Highgate Television, a division of Learning Corporation of America and Robert Keeshan Associates, Inc., for broadcast on the CBS television network.

To Brenner. A.M.F.

1

It was seven twenty-five in the morning and Bertram Cummings was lying in a tangle of sheets and blankets, staring at the cracks on his ceiling, and waiting for his alarm clock to go off.

Bertram was always awake before the alarm went off. It didn't matter how early he had to get up, his eyes snapped open at least ten minutes before the alarm clock bleeped at him to start the day.

Start the day.

For some reason, this morning, he dreaded the thought of it. True, he was hungry and by getting up he could eat. But he would also have to dress and organize his books and collect his milk money, and all of this led him in one direction and one direction only.

School.

Ugh, he thought as he reached back behind his head, took the pillow, and covered his face.

It wasn't that high school had been so bad up till now. In fact, it had been quite pleasant. Bertram's favorite subject was science, and at Masters High School you were allowed to take two science courses a semester. For Bertram, taking biology and general science was like being let out of school for two hours a day.

But for those other hours of the day he was very aware of being in school. He was very aware of being surrounded by currents of people charging through the halls. Whether they were the confident upperclassman jocks or the swaying cheerleaders, or even the people his own age who belonged to their tight groups of friends, Bertram knew he just didn't fit in. He was a single drop of oil in a tubful of water.

But then he hadn't really fit in in grade school either, or junior high. He had tried to make friends by joining clubs or getting on committees or getting involved in sports, but one by one, all these efforts had ended in disaster.

Things were fine as long as he just went with the flow. But the minute he tried to *do* anything it was like putting a target on his back and asking to get shot down. Like the time in seventh grade he offered to arrange refreshments for a class party. It had been up to him to get punch, cake, cookies, and potato chips for everyone. He was so excited about getting the job that he went out and bought everything two weeks before he had to. And there wasn't enough room in his refrigerator to keep it all, so he called a guy in his math class, Charley O'Donnell, because he knew Charley's parents had a spare refrigerator in the basement. He asked Charley if he could keep the stuff there and Charley said fine and everything was dandy until—on the morning of the party—Bertram went over to Charley's and found that every cookie, every potato chip, every piece of cake, and every last drop of punch were gone. Charley later told him his little brother and sister had discovered the stuff in the refrigerator the night before and polished it off without telling anyone.

It was right before school, so there was no time to go to the store, and no one he could call. Bertram ran home and got a half a box of Oreos, a bag of stale Doritos and a jar of Tang. Silently he presented these refreshments to the class, and as humiliating experiences go, this wasn't so bad. No one really said anything, everyone just stared in disbelief. No one touched the Oreos. Or the Doritos. Or the Tang. The party ended after about twenty minutes, and no one asked Bertram to explain, so he didn't, but walking out of the classroom later, he heard someone mutter "That's what happens when you treat nerds like people."

That was the last time Bertram had ever volunteered to do anything at school.

But now he was in high school, surrounded by new people, and more than once he thought about trying again. Occasionally a teacher would say "Would somebody like to—?" and Bertram would think about it, consider the consequences of putting himself on the line, and remain silent.

This was fine for the beginning months of the school year, when all the freshmen were getting their bearings, but now it was almost November—clubs were formed, events were being announced, and Bertram had begun to get that certain feeling in the pit of his stomach, that queasy feeling that told him something horrible was going to happen.

He rolled over on his side and saw the digital numbers of the clock change from 7:29 to 7:30. The alarm bleeped. Bertram listened to it for a moment, then reached over and shut it off.

A new day was beginning.

Yippee.

"Are you sure you don't want me to make you breakfast?" his mother asked. Bertram was peering into the refrigerator, looking for the peach jelly. His mother, dressed for work, was next to the kitchen counter.

"No, Mom," Bertram said. "I can do it." He found the jelly, pulled it out, and set it on the counter next to the bread.

"You're just going to have toast?" she asked.

"I always have toast."

"Not when I made you breakfast." Bertram's mother had started working at an insurance office in the summer. She hadn't made breakfast since mid-July, which was fine with Bertram. He enjoyed being alone in the morning and puttering around the kitchen. The house was still, filled with light. Outside, the world glistened with promise. He had the time to mull things over, or do homework, or listen to the radio. It was a good time of day.

"You could have some eggs or instant oatmeal," his mother continued.

"Mom, I'm in high school now," Bertram said, getting the bread out.

"Oh," his mother said with a smile. "Of course."

"Anyway, I'm late. It's almost eight o'clock."

Mrs. Cummings looked at her watch. "So am I." She leaned over and kissed Bertram on the cheek, then ran her fingers through his hair and looked at him. "Are you feeling all right?"

"Yeah," Bertram said. "Why?"

"You've been kind of quiet lately."

There was no way Bertram could explain the feeling

of dread that he had, the feeling that as the year wore on he was getting closer and closer to total disaster. So he just smiled and said, "Haven't had much to say, I guess."

His mother smiled. "Okay. Just checking." She crossed over to the hall and picked up her briefcase. "Your dad left milk money on the table. Don't forget it."

"Okay," Bertram said, dropping bread into the toaster. "Bye."

Bertram heard the door open and close, then crossed around to the other side of the counter and began filling in the answers on his history exercise.

Suddenly he smelled something burning. At first he thought it might be the neighbors burning their garbage again, but the sting of smoke in his eyes told him it might be closer.

He looked across the counter and saw smoke curling up out of the toaster, filling the room.

He jumped up off the stool, ran around to the toaster, picked up a paper towel, and began fanning furiously at the smoke. It was spreading out as it hit the ceiling and hanging in a cloud over the room. Bertram coughed and wiped his glasses and fanned faster. As he was doing this, the edge of the paper towel happened to brush against one of the coils, and within seconds he was holding a small torch.

He screamed and tossed it into the smoky air. The burning paper was totally engulfed by flame as it blew across the counter and collided with a whole stack of paper towels, setting them on fire.

Bertram screamed again and lunged for the sink as a horrible fantasy flashed before his eyes: the toaster exploding, setting the curtains on fire, the curtains igniting the walls, causing the electric wires to short and burn, the superstructure of the house succumbing to fire and, hours later, Bertram standing in front of a pile of charred wood that had once been his house. His parents would come home and demand an explanation, and when Bertram couldn't give one, his father would mumble, "Well, that's what happens when you let nerds make toast."

At the sink, Bertram filled a glass with water and threw it on the burning paper. Then he yanked the toaster plug. The smoke didn't stop pouring out, but at least he could be reasonably sure the toaster wouldn't explode.

A few sparks on the damp paper towels continued to crackle; Bertram threw another glass of water on them, and they went out with a final *hiss.* He picked up the toaster, flipped it upside down, and shook it over the sink. Black crumbly pieces of bread fell out.

"Wow," he mumbled to himself. Then he decided that that wasn't a significant enough thing to say. *"God,"* he said, and set about cleaning up the mess.

Maybe this was it, he thought. Maybe this was the terrible thing I thought would happen and now it's over, now I'm free and clear. But as he wiped the last piece of burned paper off the countertop, he knew deep down that this wasn't so. What had happened today was just the start of what was *about* to happen, and what was *about* to happen was that he was going to get caught up in . . . something.

He pitched the wet, dirty paper towels into the wastebasket and looked at his watch. It read 8:15.

School started at 8:15, and it was a ten-minute walk between there and his house.

Bertram sighed out loud, gathered his knapsack, gym

bag, coat, and milk money, and ran out of the house. Life is what you make it, he told himself. This won't be a bad day unless I let it be.

He nodded to himself and straightened up as he walked along through tingly October air.

Then it hit him. A tap on the top of his head.

No, he thought. Please, no.

Another. *Plop.* And another. *Plip.*

Bertram didn't look up. He didn't have to. He knew what was coming: the sound of thunder, booming in the horizon, followed by a million rain pellets being dumped out of the sky.

And right onto the head of Bertram Cummings.

2

"You're late, Bertram," Miss Henzel said.

Bertram headed right to his seat, dripping a wet trail behind him. He hadn't had time to get to his locker so he was still burdened by his coat, knapsack, and gym bag. He squeezed between two rows of seats, managing to knock a girl's books to the floor. She rolled her eyes and picked them up. A few people chuckled.

Bertram sat, stuffed his things under his seat, and wiggled out of his drenched coat. He was out of breath and sweating. His hair felt pasted to his head.

Miss Henzel, the English teacher, got up from her desk and picked up a stack of tests.

"I have your exams corrected, class," she began, "and I can't say I'm very pleased. No, not pleased at all."

Miss Henzel was about fifty, tall and stooped, and so long as Bertram had been in her class, had *never* been pleased with the results of an exam.

When she got to his row, Bertram was able to make out some of the grades of the people around him. Jeff Newhouse, right in front of him, got a C minus; Cheryl

Smith, on his left, got a D; Bill Bentley, on his right, got a B minus.

Miss Henzel laid Bertram's test down. He turned it over and was delighted but not completely surprised that he'd gotten an A plus. He smiled to himself. It might not be such a bad day after all.

Feeling someone looking over his shoulder, he turned and saw Annie Crapshaw staring at his exam. Her eyebrows were arched angrily and she was sneering.

"What a nerd," she said.

Bertram noticed that her grade was a D plus.

"I'll bet it's the only A plus in the whole class," Annie said, just loud enough for everyone in the room to hear. They all turned and stared at Bertram; everyone had the same expression as Annie.

Bertram flipped his test over so no one could see, then sank down in his seat.

It figured, Bertram thought, that on a day like today he would have gym class.

Bertram had gym on Monday, Wednesday, and Friday, and it was the main reason that Tuesday and Thursday were his favorite days of the week. (Not counting Saturday and Sunday, which he thought of more as rest periods than days.) Gym was to him *the* most excruciating torture ever devised. There was not a single sport at which he excelled, not one exercise that didn't nearly kill him, and most of all, not one person in the class whom he liked.

Today promised to be a doozy.

The sport was wrestling.

"Okay, guys, we're going to pair off," said Mr. Donovan, the gym teacher. Mr. Donovan was a big man. Bertram thought he was a little fat to be a gym teacher, as he probably couldn't do half the sports he instructed the class in.

The class, made up entirely of guys today—since none of the girls wanted to wrestle and had opted for volleyball instead—was lined up in front of the wrestling mats. Bertram had thought briefly about asking Mr. Donovan if he could join the girls for volleyball, but then decided he wouldn't be able to bear the humiliation (not to mention the fact that he was a lousy volleyball player).

Mr. Donovan read off the pairs of guys to wrestle together. When he got to Bertram's name he paused briefly, looked at Bertram, then paired him with Olaf Anderson.

Bertram felt an enormous lump swell up in his throat. Obviously, Mr. Donovan had made a mistake. Olaf Anderson, though not terrifyingly huge, had just finished a season as one of the school's top wrestlers. He'd gone all the way to the state finals, where he was beaten in a savage battle with a senior named Liu Chen.

Bertram had read all about it in the sports section of the school newspaper. He had read all about how Olaf and Chen had batted heads, twisted one another's arms, and thrown one another to the ground.

Bertram leaned forward in line and looked over at Olaf. He wasn't much taller than Bertram, but his skin seemed absolutely packed with muscles. Even his face had muscles. They twitched as he turned and smiled at Bertram. It was not a kind smile.

"Okay, let's go!" Mr. Donovan yelled, then blew his whistle.

All the guys moved onto the mat in pairs. Bertram saw Olaf pick an empty spot. He had already snapped on his headgear. Bertram still had his in his hand.

"What are you waiting for, Cummings?" Mr. Donovan asked.

"It's just that—" Bertram said. "I mean, are you sure you want me and Olaf . . . ?"

"That's who I paired you with, isn't it?"

"—yes, sir—"

"Well, then, onto the mat, boy, onto the mat." Mr. Donovan blew his whistle and Bertram hustled onto the mat. He strapped the headgear on. It felt awkward and hurt his ears.

Olaf looked at him. "You've got it on backwards," he said.

Bertram nodded, pulled it off, and put it on the right way. It still felt uncomfortable.

Olaf immediately assumed a crouch. He reminded Bertram of a werewolf. "Ready?" Olaf said.

"I guess," Bertram mumbled, but before he could get into his crouch, Olaf had rushed at him, grappled his arms around his middle, lifted him in the air, and dumped him flat on his back.

Then he cradled his right arm under Bertram's knees, wrapped his left arm around his neck, and rolled him over onto his stomach.

Bertram would have gasped, but he had absolutely no air. In minutes he knew he would be dead. But Olaf probably wouldn't know for hours. He'd just keep flipping and bending him into all sorts of interesting positions until he got bored. Then he would leave Bertram's mutilated body on the mat for the janitors to clean up.

Now Olaf was moving in for the kill. He gripped Bertram's left arm, lifted him once again off the mat, and dropped him once again on his back. Then he flopped down, slamming his hard, heaving chest into Bertram's ribs. Finally, he flattened out Bertram's shoulders.

Mr. Donovan stood over them. "Hey, I think you got a pin there, Olaf," he said.

"Yep," Olaf said, then got up off Bertram.

"What do you say, Bertram?" Mr. Donovan said. "That Olaf's some wrestler, huh?"

Bertram felt like a piece of paper at the bottom of a wastebasket. He took a breath. It hurt.

"Yes sir," Bertram wheezed. "Some wrestler."

Gym class finally ended after two more wrestling bouts—one with Steve Shepard, who pinned Bertram in two minutes, the other with Carl Forggia, who pinned him in one—and an embarrassing session in the weight room, in which Bertram strained to bench-press forty pounds.

Limping down the hall afterwards with a small Curad over his left eye (put on by Mr. Donovan after Bertram walked into a closed door, unable to see it because his glasses had been left in his gym locker), he wanted nothing more at that moment than to just lie down and go to sleep.

He stopped for a moment and leaned against the nearest wall, rubbing his eyes. What he failed to notice was that he was standing right next to a water fountain. And that a kid was bending down to use it.

The kid, not seeing Bertram, pressed the fountain's foot pedal and sent a stream of water into Bertram's face.

The water hit Bertram like an icy and unexpected slap. It dribbled down his face, his neck, and into the collar of his shirt. Moments later, he felt the wetness spread across his chest and stomach and into his underpants.

"Sorry," the kid said, taking his drink then moving on down the hall.

"It's okay," Bertram replied. He stood where he was a moment, afraid if he moved the water would begin to run down the legs of his pants.

"Hey, Bertram," he heard from behind.

Bertram turned and saw his best friend, Dalton Surewood, coming down the hall. Dalton was tall, confident, good-looking, and a great dresser. Often, when he looked at him, Bertram was puzzled as to why they were such good friends. It might have been different if Dalton got the sort of grades Bertram did, or was able to talk on his level about science, physics, and computers. But Dalton was a completely average student and quite happy to stay that way. If talk of anything specifically technical came up between the two, it was Bertram who talked, explained, and drew diagrams; Dalton sat, smiled, and occasionally nodded politely.

But between them there seemed to be an understanding. Dalton never minded that when he played one-on-one basketball with Bertram he had to give him a twenty-four point lead, and Bertram never minded that when it came to exam time, Dalton would ask to be tutored in whatever subject he had sluffed off on that term.

Dalton came up to Bertram and noticed the water dripping down his face.

"Workin' up a good sweat there, I see," he said with a crooked grin.

"Very funny," Bertram said, wiping his glasses. "Watch me die laughing."

Dalton reached into his pocket, pulled out a handkerchief and handed it to Bertram. Bertram cleaned off his glasses with it, wiped his face, and dried his neck.

"Thanks."

"What happened to your head?" Dalton asked, pointing to the bandage over Bertram's eye.

"What always happens to my head?" Bertram said. "Gym class."

"Oh, yeah, it's wrestling this week. I guess that's not your sport, either."

"I have yet to find one that is," Bertram said. He handed the handkerchief back to Dalton. "Are you going down to the library?"

"Yeah. You?"

"No, I don't think so. I thought I might—" Bertram stopped. Through a crowd of people across the hall, something seemed to reach out and grab his attention. No, not some*thing*. Some*one*.

And not just anyone.

But her.

Her with the fine, fair skin, the shimmering blond hair, the graceful dancer's walk. Her with the emerald eyes and the tiny bent nose and the clear, even smile. Her who weeks ago had stepped out of a crowd very much like this one and taken hold (as she was doing now) of all of Bertram's senses, shaken them into a jumble, and when she had walked out of sight, left him limp and dazed and dazzled.

Her who was now walking into the school library.

"Bertram?" Dalton said. "Yoo hoo. Bertram."

Bertram shook himself a little. "Hm?"

"I said I was going to the library. You coming or not?"

"The library," Bertram said. "Absolutely. Let's go to the library."

3

"Who is she?" Dalton asked.

She was sitting about twenty feet from where he and Dalton were, curled up on a couch reading the latest issue of *Modern Dance*.

"Louise Baker," Bertram answered, not taking his eyes off her for one second. "I'm in love."

"Does she know you're alive?"

"Does anyone?"

"I don't suppose you've tried anything outrageous and daring—like talking to her."

Bertram let his attention drift from Louise a moment and looked at Dalton. "Do you think I'm crazy?"

"It's better than spending all your time gawking at her with your mouth open."

"My mouth is *not* open when I gawk!" Bertram yelled.

Mrs. Dellaco, the librarian, looked up from her desk and scowled at Bertram.

Bertram said again, more quietly, "My mouth is *not*

open when I gawk. And anyway, who says that just because I'm in love with her she has to know?"

"I've been looking at you for the last twenty minutes," Dalton said. "You look just like this . . ." Opening his eyes wide, he let his mouth sag open and his tongue hang out.

"I do not!" Bertram yelled, and this time Mrs. Dellaco put her finger over her lips and shushed him.

Dalton said, "Hey, Bertram, look—what would be the harm in just saying hello to the girl? Starting up a conversation? Getting to be friends?"

"Friends? You think that's so easy?"

"I don't see what the big deal is."

"Of course *you* don't. You have girls hanging around you all the time."

Dalton rolled his eyes. "Oh, I do not."

"I mean the only time I ever get to talk to girls," Bertram continued, "is when they're around you. And that's only to say 'Well it was nice meeting you, but Dalton and I really have to be going.' "

"Talking to girls isn't any harder than talking to me."

"Sometimes talking to you isn't so easy," Bertram said with a smile.

"Oh, right," Dalton said.

The bell rang. Dalton stood up and started collecting his books. Bertram sat where he was. He had a perfect view of Louise getting up off the couch, returning the magazine to its rack, and walking out of the library.

"You doing anything after school?" Dalton asked.

"Yeah, I'm working on my science project," Bertram answered. He stood up and slung his knapsack over his shoulder. "I'm almost finished with it."

"Oh, yeah? Can I come over and take a look?"

"Sure. Why don't you drop by around four."

They headed out of the library and into the streams of people walking down the hall.

"Okay," Dalton said. "See you then."

"See you," Bertram said and hurried to his next class.

Bertram had good reason to hurry to his next class. Not only was it general science, his favorite subject, taught by Mr. Barnes, his favorite teacher, but Louise Baker was in it.

He had prayed that he would be picked as her lab partner. But as luck and the fates would have it, she sat all the way across the room from him. But still, to have Louise in the same class was lucky enough for any man.

Bertram hadn't mentioned this to Dalton because he knew if Dalton were to find out he saw her every day he would be nagged mercilessly about talking to her. As it was, Bertram was content to just sit and look at her. Well, not content exactly. He was *satisfied* to just sit and look at her and *satisfied* that by just sitting and looking he had little chance of making a fool of himself.

Bertram walked into the classroom and made his way over to his lab table. On the way he glanced at Louise's seat and saw that she hadn't come yet. Bertram always preferred it if he got to science a little before Louise, because that way Mike Godey would be finished with him by the time she got there.

"Hey, hey, hey," Mike Godey barked as Bertram sat down on his stool, "looks like Bertram hurt himself. What happened, guy? Get mugged by a midget?"

Bertram said nothing as he laid his knapsack on the black tabletop and tried to ignore what he knew was coming next. All roses have thorns, he thought to himself, and my science class has Mike Godey.

"He never answers me," Mike said to Dennis, who sat

next to him. Then he said to Chuck, who sat across from him, "I try to talk to him all the time and he never says nothin' back."

Mike Godey wasn't a tough guy, exactly, or a burnout either. And he wasn't a class clown or a teacher's pet, and he sure wasn't a brain. But Mike was two things that made everyone in a room notice him: he was loud and he was cocky. If he had something to say, he said it, stood behind it, and never backed down, right or wrong. (It probably helped him some that Chuck and Dennis, his two best friends, were constantly at his side.) And nobody ever seemed to disagree with Mike (except teachers, but this never fazed him), and nobody seemed to mind that he never knew when to shut up. He was a *part* of the school and the student life in a way that Bertram knew he wasn't. Bertram knew he was smarter than Godey, easier to get along with, and to some degree, even better-looking. (It wasn't that Mike was bad-looking, but he seemed to wear the same expression all the time—as if he'd just swallowed an onion whole.) So why was Mike Godey tolerated and Bertram Cummings humiliated?

"Well," Mike said, shaking his head at Bertram, "I guess when the midget mugged him he musta stole his tongue." Chuck and Dennis, as if on cue, laughed. A few others did also.

Bertram sat on his rising anger. There were any number of comebacks he could fire at Godey. "My tongue and your brain," came to mind immediately, followed by "Anybody who'd steal *your* tongue ought to get a medal," and "That wasn't a midget—it was your old man." But as usual, Bertram said nothing. Why start trouble? he thought.

Just then Louise strode in. As usual, the very act of

her walking sent Bertram's head into a spin, made the insides of his ears buzz, and sent a gentle tickle along his ribs.

She plopped her dance bag down next to her stool and sat, never once looking at Bertram. She whispered something to her lab partner, Andrea, and they both giggled. Bertram longed to giggle with Louise Baker. He would even have settled for a small chuckle, a quick smile.

The back door of the classroom opened and Mr. Barnes, a tall square-shouldered black man in his early thirties, walked to his desk. He slid on a pair of half-glasses and opened a textbook.

As always, Barnes peered at Bertram over the glasses and the two exchanged a smile just before the class began. This had been their ritual ever since Bertram had stayed after class one day to chat with Mr. Barnes about an extra-credit project. They had ended up talking until after six o'clock.

Barnes picked up the text and began reading. "What is the possibility of life on other planets?" his voice boomed. "This is a question that has caused debate for many years. . . ."

Several hours later, Dalton Surewood was lying on Bertram's bed, watching his friend as he sat hunched over a wooden workbench, screwing together what looked like a portable television set. This was, Dalton knew, THE BIG PROJECT. This was what Bertram had been working day and night on since September; this was going to be the project to end all projects, the greatest scientific breakthrough ever made by a fourteen-year-old. The only thing he didn't know was *what* the project was exactly. Bertram never discussed projects while he was in the middle of them. He thought it was bad luck. And Dalton could never make head or tail of any of the drawings, notes, and graphs spread out across the room. He didn't ask about the television screen, computer board, and radar dish, because he knew he'd never get an answer, just a mumble and a shrug.

Most of Bertram's previous inventions had been interesting but not very practical. When Dalton had first met him in fifth grade Bertram was working on a rocket that would transport mice. It worked all right; so well that after they launched it they never saw the rocket or the mice again. Early in seventh grade Bertram turned in a class science project having to do with remote-control kitchen appliances. A housewife, he had said, could be shopping while she was vacuuming by remote control. But in his demonstration at school the vacuum cleaner malfunctioned and ate Laurie Fingerman's shoes.

Bertram straightened up from the bench and stretched. "Okay," he said. "Done."

"I don't believe it," Dalton said. "After months of work, weeks of complete secrecy, it's finally finished?"

"And you can be the first to see it."

Dalton bounced up off the bed and sat down next to Bertram at the workbench. "Okay, show it to me."

"Not here," Bertram said. He was fiddling with the television set. He appeared to be adjusting the picture, yet there was no picture. "Go into my mom's room and turn on the TV."

Dalton shrugged, got up, and left the room. When he got to Mrs. Cummings's room, he switched on the TV.

"Any particular channel?" he called.

"No," Bertram called back.

Dalton left it where it was: channel 5, a rerun of *Gilligan's Island*. He waited. Nothing happened.

Dalton was starting to shout "Hey, Bert" when all at once the image on the screen began to flutter and the sound began to die out. Then the picture disappeared altogether, but the screen didn't go blank. Another image was coming through. It took a second or two to set, but when it did, Dalton and Bertram were face to face. But Bertram's face was on television.

Dalton, so shocked he couldn't think of a single appropriate thing to say, just sat there, shaking his head.

"Well," Bertram's voice crackled over the TV, "what do you think?"

Dalton replied, "It's absolutely—" Then he realized Bertram was two rooms away, still unable to hear what he said. He shouted, "It's absolutely unbelievable!"

Bertram's image smiled even wider. "I can do this to any TV within a five-mile radius," he said. "It's just a matter of honing in on the right frequency."

"I can't believe I'm looking at this! I really can't!"

Bertram continued, "I can do it to a lot of sets at once or just one at a time. Come on back, I'll show you."

"Is it okay if I switch off the set?"

"What?" Bertram's image asked.

Dalton spoke louder. "I said, Is it okay if I switch off the set?"

"Yeah, sure."

Dalton punched the OFF button and his friend's face flickered from sight.

Back in his room Bertram was sitting in front of a small, black movie camera mounted on a tripod. He was adjusting something inside it as Dalton came back in.

"Fabulous," Dalton was muttering. "Absolutely fabulous."

Bertram moved from the camera over to a small computer keyboard, which was hooked up to the television set on the shelf. He typed for a few seconds on the keyboard, then waited as a computerized map began to take shape on the screen. The map included streets, blocks, houses, and buildings.

"That's our neighborhood," Dalton said.

"That's right," Bertram said. "See?" He pointed. "Here's my house in the center, your house, the school . . ."

"How come all the houses are gray except that one?" Dalton pointed to a bright red image of a house in the left corner of the map.

"That's *her* house," Bertram said with reverence.

"Her?" Then it came to him. "Oh, Louise."

Bertram nodded. Just the mention of her name had glazed his eyes, slackened his jaw.

"Boy," Dalton said, "have you ever got it bad."

"I had an idea. I was thinking of broadcasting to Louise's TV real late at night—maybe while she's sleeping—and saying something like 'You love Bertram, Bertram is the only man for you . . .'"

Dalton sighed and rubbed his eyes.

"'. . . when you wake up today, you will *live* for Bertram, die for Bertram, long for Bertram.'" He stopped suddenly and scratched his ear. "Bertram," he said slowly. Then again: "Ber-tram." He paused. "What a stupid name."

Dalton looked at him. "What are you talking about?"

"The problem is my name. Bertram. Bertram isn't a name. Jack is a name. Dave is a name. Bertram is a curse."

"Oh, come on."

"No, I'm serious. I think I've hit on a real discovery here. The reason people don't want to talk to me is because of my name. Who wants to say 'Hi, Bertram' when they can say 'Hi, Steve' or 'Hi, Bill'?"

"The problem is not your name—" Dalton began.

"You're right, it's not the only problem. The other problem is that I'm short. If I was just a little taller. Not a lot, but tall enough to look people in the eye instead of the throat."

"The problem is your attitude," Dalton said. He leaned forward in his chair and played with some of the buttons on the keyboard.

"Don't touch," Bertram said.

Dalton stopped playing with the keyboard. "I mean you must be the smartest guy I know. I don't know anybody else your age who's ever invented anything like this. This could be a real technological break-through. You might even get on the cover of *Popular Mechanics.*"

"Oh, come on."

"Really. And you're sitting here telling me what a nerd you think you are."

"It's not what I think, it's what everybody else thinks," Bertram said. "And it's not even what everybody else thinks." He pointed to the red house. "It's what *she* thinks."

"How do you know what she thinks? You don't even know what her voice sounds like. You have yet to carry on a simple conversation with her."

Bertram started playing with a loose screw on the workbench. "Yeah, well . . ."

"Yeah, well nothing. Either try and talk to the girl or forget about her and move on."

"But what if something stupid happens? Like I forget my own name or something."

Dalton clapped his hand on his friend's shoulder for reassurance. "I'll be right there to remind you. We can even write it on your hand if you want."

Bertram smiled. He hit a button on the keyboard and the image of Louise's little red house flashed brightly.

"Okay, Louise," Bertram said. "Ready, or not, here I come."

4

They were crouched behind the library's enormous globe of the earth, eyes locked on Louise, who was once again stretched out on the couch in the library, reading a copy of *Modern Dance*.

"You really think I should go up and introduce myself? Just like that?"

"It's worked for hundreds of years."

"I can't do it."

"What do you mean?"

"I mean—I mean I want to send flowers first. Or candy. Or a book."

"A *book?*"

"I don't know what I'm saying. Let's get out of here." Bertram turned and started to get up. Dalton wrapped his fingers around his arm and pulled him back down.

"Last night you were so gung ho for this," he said.

"Last night I was sitting in my room."

"Well, now you're sitting in the library. And so is she. And she's alone."

"She's not alone, she's reading. I don't want to bother her."

"She's reading because she's bored. She's reading because she's waiting for someone witty, good-looking, and charming to come up and talk to her. You."

Bertram gulped. Then he looked around, searching for any excuse not to go through with this. "Mike Godey's here," he said. He pointed to a nearby table, where Godey, Dennis, and Chuck were all playing poker.

"So?"

"So he hates me. Everytime he sees me he makes a crack or throws something. He'll mess it all up."

"He's in the middle of a poker game. He won't even notice."

"You sure?"

Dalton leaned forward, getting a good look. "He's got a royal flush. No way is he gonna notice you."

Bertram took a deep, calming breath. "Okay," he said. "Okay, I'm gonna do it. I'm really gonna do it."

"Right. Now just remember what we rehearsed."

Bertram nodded and stood up. His knees felt as if they'd been joined together with rubber bands. He took a step, then another, all the time keeping his eyes on Louise. As he walked toward her, he whispered to himself what he and Dalton had worked out last night: "Hi, my name's Bertram. Don't we have a class together?" Then in a slightly deeper voice: "Hi, my name's Bertram. Don't we have a class together?"

Mike Godey, who had just passed the deal to Chuck, happened to look up and see Bertram as he walked by. "That nerd," he said.

"Who?" Chuck asked.

"Him," Mike pointed. "Cummings. I swear he is the biggest—Oh, my God!"

Dennis looked up. "What?"

Mike said, "I don't believe it."

"What is it?" Chuck asked.

"He's going over to talk to Louise Baker."

Dennis and Chuck both laughed. Then Dennis said, "Hey, you want me to hit him with a spit wad?"

"Are you kidding?" Mike said. "He's gonna screw it up all by himself. Just watch."

Bertram had now made it to the edge of Louise's couch. He paused, then cleared his throat.

Louise remained immersed in *Modern Dance.*

Bertram cleared his throat louder, and this time she looked up. Her gorgeous green eyes cut through Bertram like a torch, and he once again had that prickly hot feeling all over.

Louise blinked.

Okay, Bertram thought, this is it—talk.

He opened his mouth. He moved his mouth. He prayed for something to come out.

"Eeuuuyuh," he managed.

Louise cocked her head politely.

Bertram tried again. "Hhheee . . ." He cleared his throat and faked a cough. What was wrong with him? Simple English, that's all it took. A few words strung together. Maybe a sentence. Was that asking too much? He summoned all the discipline he knew, every bit of concentration he could manage.

"Hi," he muttered.

"Hi," Louise said back, and smiled brightly.

This so shocked Bertram that he was completely unable to remember any other word in the language. She had actually spoken. She had smiled. Brightly. What did it all mean? What was happening? Did this mean she actually liked him, and had liked him all along? Or was she just being polite, just stringing him along until someone better came along? It was too much to deal with all at one time. He would have to go away and think.

"Well," he muttered, "bye."

Mike Godey observed Bertram as he backed away from Louise. An idea suddenly flashed into his head, and as Bertram started to walk past—eyes still locked on Louise—Mike stuck his foot out.

Bertram felt his ankles collide with something, and before he was able to do anything he was tumbling backwards, his hands scrambling to grab onto something and his glasses flying off his face.

He hit the carpet with a thump, amazed that it really didn't hurt that much. He blinked and started looking around for his glasses, then realized someone was looking down at him. Bertram blinked again and tried to focus.

A familiar voice laughed and said, "Okay, Bertram, now the next step is to tell her your name. Lemme help you out. It starts with the same letter as Birdbrain."

Several people laughed. Bertram knew that the voice, and the foot that had tripped him, belonged to Mike.

Something dark and fuzzy was dangled in front of his face. His glasses. He tried to grab at them but they were pulled away.

Just then the class bell rang. Bertram heard people getting up and shuffling into the hall and saw vague shapes pass before him.

Dalton, who had watched the whole thing from behind the globe, walked over to Mike and said, "Give him back the glasses, Godey."

Mike looked up at Dalton and grinned. "Yeah, sure," he said, and flipped the spectacles into the air. They landed on Bertram's chest. "Come on, you guys," he said to Chuck and Dennis. Dennis gathered up the cards and the three strode out of the library.

Bertram slipped the glasses back on and propped himself up on his elbows. Dalton was sitting in a chair, looking down at him.

"I don't want to hear one word about this," Bertram said.

"C'mon," Dalton said.

"Not one word. This was the most humiliating, degrading experience of my life."

Dalton shrugged. "So? It happens. At least you've broken the ice with her."

"Broken the ice?" Bertram shook his head. "Not only do I freeze up completely but then I trip and I let that—that Cro-Magnon Godey make an idiot out of me." He looked at his watch and moaned. "And now I've got science. And Mike and Louise are both in it."

"You're going to go, aren't you?"

"What's the point? It'd all be just a rerun of what happened here."

"It doesn't have to be," Dalton said. "The first thing to do is take care of Godey. Okay, maybe he's a little stronger than you and a lot meaner. But you're smarter. In every single way, especially science. Why, if he was to so much as open his mouth in that class you could make dog food out of him."

Bertram's face brightened. "And then I'd show Louise that I'm not the kind of guy who gets pushed around and takes it."

"Right!"

"Okay," Bertram said, his enthusiasm building. "Okay, I'll do it."

And with that Bertram sucked up a chestful of confidence and marched out of the library.

Mr. Barnes had just finished reading a section of the textbook on the possibility of life in other parts of our solar system when Mike Godey raised his hand.

"Yes, Mike?" Mr. Barnes said.

"Uh, I'd just like to maybe add something here," Mike said.

"Go ahead."

"Well, maybe this is gonna sound weird, but I've seen a UFO."

Mr. Barnes's eyebrows went up in amazement; a few people in the class laughed or smiled to themselves.

Barnes tread carefully around Mike. He was a troublemaker who often disrupted class, but also a bright kid. He seemed sincere enough at the moment to be ignoring the sneers around him.

"You're sure about this?" Mr. Barnes asked.

"Absolutely."

"When was this?"

"It was about a week ago, and I'm serious. I was outside, riding my bike. It was nighttime and I looked up and saw it and it was"—Mike's face was filled with the wonder of the memory—"it was incredible! It was perfectly round, saucer-shaped, and it was moving really fast, cutting right turns, then cutting back again. I couldn't believe it."

No one in the class was laughing now. Everyone was taken with Mike's apparent sincerity, his complete belief in what he was saying.

Bertram picked up his pen and drew a saucer shape on a page of his notebook. Sticking out of the top of the saucer he drew a little green man, who was saying "Hi, Mike" and waving.

"What did it finally do?" Barnes asked.

Mike said, "Well, I rode home to tell my dad about it, but by the time I got there it was just . . . gone."

Bertram looked over at Louise. Along with everyone else, she was completely immersed in what Mike was saying. Bertram drew a small heart in the corner of his page.

"So," Mr. Barnes said, "you believe in life on other planets?"

"Are you kiddin'? Absolutely."

Next to the Louise heart, Bertram drew a tiny self-portrait, a stick figure with glasses with a bubble over his head, saying "Hey, Louise, over here!"

Barnes was quiet for a moment, fiddling with his half-glasses and frowning slightly. "Let's get another opinion on this," he said. "Bertram, what do you think?"

Bertram was expecting this. Barnes often called on him to give a particular scientific point of view. Bertram looked up from his doodling and pretended to be surprised. "You mean about what Mike said?"

"Yes."

"Well," Bertram began, picking his words carefully, "when you look at something like this, you have to take into account all factors."

Mike snapped his head around and gave Bertram his sourest look. "Waddayou think, I don't know what I saw?"

"I didn't say that. What I meant was, was it last Wednesday by any chance?"

Mike thought a moment, still eyeing Bertram as if he were a rattlesnake. "Yeah. Yeah, it was."

"And it was cloudy that night."

"Right, yeah."

Bertram folded his arms. "I saw the same thing."

A smile eight feet wide split across Mike's face and he yelled; "I was right! I was right, and the nerd even says so!" He raised his arms victoriously, laughing.

As Mike's laughter and the class's oohs and ahs died down, Bertram said, loudly but evenly; "It was the spotlight from Don's Used Car Lot bouncing off the clouds."

Mike's arms dropped. The class was once again silent.

Bertram glanced over at Louise. She was looking at him, her eyes flooded with sheer amazement. Her stare seemed to feed Bertram's confidence and he went on. "The light formed a saucer shape and—"

"Wait a minute, Cummings," Mike snapped. "Are you telling me I don't know the difference between a spotlight and a flying saucer?"

"As a matter of fact, I am," Bertram shot back.

The class exploded with laughter at this and would have gone right on, but Mr. Barnes interrupted.

"Quiet down, class," he said. "That's enough." When everyone had settled a bit, Barnes said to Bertram; "Do you want to diagram it for us?"

Bertram nodded confidently and walked up to the blackboard. There he diagramed clearly and concisely exactly how a spotlight bouncing off of some clouds could give the appearance of a glowing, fast-moving saucer.

The more he talked, the further Mike slumped over on his table, until by the end of Bertram's speech it was almost impossible to see him behind his books.

And the more Bertram talked, the more Louise's eyes seemed to fill with admiration.

Bertram drew his final diagram, set down his chalk, turned to everyone, and said; "And that is pretty much that."

Several people, including Louise, applauded.

Mike just sat right where he was, slumped down behind his books. He had disliked Bertram the way you might dislike a fly that was buzzing around your head; now he *loathed* him. "Just wait, nerd," he whispered to himself. "Just wait."

5

Mike had gotten even with nerds like Bertram plenty of times before. When Barney Katzman had called him a mental midget in sixth grade, Mike got into his locker, found his lunchbag and replaced the bologna in his sandwich with two dead mice; when Sheila Murphy had called him a wimp in front of the whole gym class, then proceeded to knock him down and beat his nose bloody, Mike went over to her house one night, climbed in through her bedroom window while she was asleep, and glued her hair to her pillow. With both Barney and Sheila, Mike made sure he was around when they found out what he did to them. He was in the cafeteria when Barney took out his sandwich, bit into it, then screamed and went running into the boys' room. And he was hiding in the bushes under Sheila's open window when she woke up and found she couldn't lift her head off the pillow, screeched and bawled for an hour as her mother cut off all her beloved golden curls.

"How ya doin', Mike?" Chuck asked, in algebra class.

"Are you still mad?" Dennis asked.

"Not anymore," Mike said, as a slow grin crept across his face.

"Uh-oh," Chuck said and looked at Dennis.

"Chuck," Mike said, "you gotta sister, don't you?"

"Yeah, her name's—"

Mike cut him off. "I want you to skip this class, go home and get me some things."

"What kind of things?"

"Some colored stationery, a red pen, a colored envelope, and some perfume. Can you get me that?"

"Yeah, I guess."

"Good. Then we'll all meet at the freshman lockers right after school."

Dennis said, "Hey, Mike, is this the thing you're gonna do to the nerd?"

Mike nodded.

"But how—?"

"Just trust me, guys. Trust old Mike." And he chuckled softly.

Dalton was just coming out of basketball practice, wiping the streams of sweat off his face with his T-shirt, when he saw Bertram coming down the hall, skipping, jumping and yelling.

"I did it!" he yelled. "I really did it!" He ran up to Dalton, took the basketball from under his arm, and began dribbling excitedly. Dalton couldn't help but grin—he hadn't seen Bertram this excited since Valentine's Day a year ago, when he'd gotten a card from Margie Whitelaw with a lipstick kiss on it. That happiness hadn't lasted long, though. Several days after he'd gotten the card, Bertram discovered it had been meant for *Bill* Cummings', who had the locker next to his.

"I take it you were a hit in science?"

Bertram continued to dribble the ball up and down the deserted hallway.

"A hit? Try smash!" He then took the ball in both hands, leaped up as if he were about to make a shot, and threw the ball against the wall. It bounced back and smacked Bertram in the chest, knocking him back a few steps.

"Better give me that before you hurt yourself," Dalton said, taking the ball back.

Bertram seemed not to notice. The two walked into the locker room together and as Dalton showered and changed, Bertram filled him in on every single detail of what had happened in science.

Dalton dried himself off. "How did Godey take it?"

Bertram shook his head and grinned. "I really got that guy. I mean it, a verbal KO."

"And Louise?"

Bertram leaned against the wall and folded his arms. "I don't know."

"What do you mean?"

"Well, she laughed—I mean, everybody did—but I thought she might talk to me after."

"She didn't?"

"No. She just sat through the rest of the class and walked out afterwards."

"Maybe she's shy. Maybe she's just waiting for you to start things off."

"But I tried that in the library."

Dalton balled up his towel, pitched it into the hamper. "Yeah. But now that you've got your confidence up you can try it in English."

"So," Bertram said as he and Dalton walked from the gym to their lockers, "you really think that Louise just sits at home, hoping and praying I'll call?"

"I wouldn't go quite that far."

"But you think it's actually possible that all this time she's been thinking the same stuff about me that I've been thinking about her?"

Dalton shrugged. "Possible."

"But do girls think about that stuff?"

"You mean, do they think about guys?"

"Yeah."

Dalton rolled his eyes. "Well, what else do they have to think about?"

"I don't know," Bertram said, shaking his head slowly. "Sometimes it just seems like . . . well, like they're almost not human. You know?"

"Take my word for it," Dalton said. "They are."

"I'm starting to come to that conclusion," Bertram said. "I mean, I did get Louise to laugh. And she wasn't even laughing *at* me."

"See? You're on your way."

They arrived at the freshman lockers. Dalton had gotten all his stuff from his gym locker, but Bertram had to stop off to pick up a few books. He spun the dial of his lock till it opened, and jacked up the handle. It was then that he noticed the smell: a sweet, feminine scent from close by. Bertram shook his head, thinking that he was imagining it, then took another sniff. No, there was definitely perfume in the air. But that was crazy. School had ended thirty minutes ago. He and Dalton were alone in the hall.

Bertram leaned over to where Dalton was standing and sniffed. "You wearing cologne or—something?"

Dalton made a face. "No, why would I—?" Then he

stopped and sniffed. "Hey!" He looked around behind them, then checked up and down the hall. "Wow, that smell!"

Dalton took another long sniff, following the trail of the scent like a bloodhound. He leaned left, then right, and finally ended up facing Bertram's open locker.

"It's coming from your locker," Dalton said. He reached over Bertram's head and picked up a purple envelope lying on top of his science book. As Dalton brought it down past his face, he and Bertram both caught the scent full in the nostrils.

"I guess that must be it," Dalton said.

"What is it?"

"It's addressed to you."

Bertram took the envelope. It was indeed addressed to him, in red marker, no less. He tore it open and pulled out a piece of purple stationery. There were hand-drawn hearts all over it, and the writing was big and loopy; all the i's were dotted with circles.

"It looks like it's from a girl," Dalton said, as they both leaned close together to read it. Bertram read aloud:

"Dearest Bertram,
 I'm really sorry about today in the library.
 For weeks now I've been waiting for you to
 come and talk to me and . . ."

"Jeez, you were right," Bertram said when they got to that part.

"Keep reading," Dalton said.

"and then that stupid Mike Godey had to go
 and ruin it all. What I'm trying to say is, I have
 a terrible crush on you. Could we have one

more chance? Tomorrow morning, right before the first class?

> With Much Antissipation,
> Louise Baker"

"I think . . ." Bertram murmured, "I think I'm going to faint."

Dalton took the letter and looked at it closely. "She
spelled anticipation wrong."

"What?"

"Look," Dalton said, pointing. "Anticipation isn't
spelled with two s's."

"I can't believe you!" Bertram snatched the letter
away. "This girl has just sent me a letter telling me she
has *worshiped* me from afar and you're talking about
grammar?"

"No, I'm talking about spelling."

"Will you *stop?* Don't you see that she was so . . . so
filled up with emotion that she didn't know what she
was doing?"

"You're probably right," Dalton said, then slapped
Bertram on the shoulder. "Well, congratulations. This is
probably the beginning of something really terrific."

"I just—I just can't really believe it yet." He was
staring at the letter, reading the words over and over.
"For weeks now I've been waiting." "I have a terrible
crush on you." ". . . one more chance."

"So what's your next step?" Dalton asked.

Bertram stuffed the letter into his jacket, then began
pulling books out of his locker. "I have to start getting
ready for tomorrow."

"Getting ready? What are you gonna do, rehearse a
speech?"

Bertram snapped his fingers. "That's not a bad idea.

No, what I'm going to do is . . . find the right kind of
clothes for this occasion."

Dalton shook his head. "Oh, boy."

"Not what you're thinking. I'm not going to overdo it.
It's going to be subtle. But she'll definitely notice a
change in me."

"But obviously she likes you the way you are."

"Well, with what I've got in mind, after tomorrow
morning she's going to *love* me." He slammed the
locker shut and slung his knapsack over his shoulder.
"You want to come along?"

"I think I'd better," Dalton said as they headed down
the hall together.

"Bertram," Dalton said, "I really do think—"

"What?" Bertram shouted from the bathroom.

"I said, I really do think this is overdoing it!" Dalton
shouted back. He was seated at Bertram's workbench,
flipping through an old *Spider-Man* comic book. Bertram was in the adjoining bathroom. He'd been in there
for close to twenty minutes. But that wasn't what bothered Dalton. He was used to waiting for Bertram. What
bothered Dalton was remembering the clothes Bertram had gone into the bathroom with. He had a whole
pile of them, all found in some forgotten corner of the
basement, all previously owned by Bertram's father
and uncles, a few even looking like they'd belonged to
his grandfather.

"Okay," Bertram called from the bathroom, "tell me
what you think of this."

Dalton turned around in his chair and literally felt as
if he had to squint when Bertram stepped through the
doorway.

His suit was made up of bright yellow and green

checks; his vest was tartan; his shirt was blue and white checks, and his tie blue and red checks. It was one of the suits Bertram had found in the basement.

To Dalton, he looked like a walking grid pattern.

"Well?" Bertram said, and for a moment Dalton was startled. He had forgotten there was actually a person attached to all this blazingly bright cross-hatching.

"Er," Dalton muttered.

"The color coordination is subtle," Bertram said, smiling proudly. "That's how I planned it."

"Uh, yeah," Dalton said.

"See," he said, "the green in the suit matches the green in the vest and then the blue in the vest matches the blue in the shirt, and the shirt and the tie both have blue and the tie has red, which matches the vest."

"Uh-huh," Dalton said.

"The only thing I couldn't quite get together," Bertram went on, "was to get yellow or green in the tie to match the suit. I mean, it's hard to find a tie with three colors in it."

"Yeah, yeah it is."

"So?"

"So."

"What do you think? Am I gonna knock her out?"

"Everybody who sees you will be knocked out. Or blinded."

"I know. It's great, isn't it? But I haven't definitely decided I'm gonna wear this."

A sigh of relief escaped Dalton's lips.

"I have some other stuff in here that I've put together." He slipped back into the bathroom. "Lemme show you."

Over the next hour and fifteen minutes, Bertram appeared in five different outfits. There was the sporty outfit (huge white baggy shorts, white knee socks, and a pink Lacoste shirt), the suave outfit (Bertram's grandfather's tuxedo with the arms and legs pinned up around the elbows and knees), the African outfit (safari jacket, pith helmet, and knee boots), the playboy outfit (red silk shirt, purple pants, and a gold chain), and finally the gangster outfit (bright green pinstripe suit with enormous padded shoulders and a felt hat—it had belonged to Bertram's great uncle, who had bought it in 1949 and worn it only once—in a summer stock production of *Guys and Dolls*).

"Well?" Bertram said, still dressed in the bright green pinstripe, "which one do you like best?"

"Um, well," Dalton began.

"Be brutally honest. We've got a lot to choose from."

"Well, to be brutally honest—Why don't you just go as yourself?"

"Myself?" Bertram said. He was peering quizzically at Dalton from under the huge rim of the felt hat.

"Yeah."

"But I thought you wanted me to *get* the girl."

"I do. But obviously she really likes you for who you are—and that includes the way you dress."

"But I want to really be sure . . ."

"Look," Dalton said, standing up. "How would you feel if Louise walked into school dressed like"—he groped for an appropriate image—"like a punk rock singer? Or"—he lifted the hat off Bertram's head, twirled it around on his finger, and put it on his own head—"or a gangster's moll. I mean, that wouldn't be the Louise you know. It'd be Louise acting like somebody."

"I guess what you're saying," Bertram said, "is that maybe I'm going a little too far with all this."

He unbuttoned the jacket, slid it off, and threw it on to the enormous pile of clothes on his bed. "But I've got to do something," he said, turning and looking at himself in the mirror.

Dalton looked at his watch. "Look, I've got to get going," he said. "But let me just leave you with some old but good advice."

"What's that?"

"Less is more. Believe me, Bertram, this whole thing'll work out much better if you just—take it easy."

Bertram nodded. "Take it easy."

Dalton reached for his coat. "Relax."

"Relax. Right."

"Just . . . play it cool. Play it casual." He headed for the door.

"Play it casual," Bertram said, trying to stand casually. Then he suddenly snapped his fingers and straightened up. "I've got it! Casual!"

"Right."

"Thanks, Dalton. Thanks a lot. You've been a big help." He ran past Dalton, out of the room and into the hall.

"Where are you going?"

"Down to the basement. I know there's something casual down there and I'm going to find it if it takes me all night!"

And with that, he whizzed down the stairs and was gone. Dalton shook his head and rubbed his eyes.

6

"Good morning, son," Bertram's father said as he passed his room the next morning.

"Hi, Dad," Bertram said as he pulled on his pants. He buttoned them at the waist and began adjusting the belt. His father stuck his head in the door.

"Where'd you get the pants?" he asked.

"Uh . . . from down in the basement."

"The basement?"

"Yeah."

"You sure they're not—a little too big for you?"

"Maybe a little." He had pulled the belt to the last notch and they still felt as if they were going to drop down around his knees if he took a step.

"Is this for school?" Mr. Cummings asked, stepping into the room. "Are you supposed to dress up in period clothes or something?"

"Period clothes?"

"Clothes from a long time ago," he said.

"Oh, no," Bertram said, fiddling with the belt. "I'm just trying to make an impression."

"An impression."

"On a girl."

Mr. Cummings nodded and said, "Ah. I see." He then reached over and gave the pants' waist a slight tug. "Maybe if we put a few safety pins on these. Just to keep them from sliding down too far."

Bertram looked down and nodded. "Yeah," he said slowly. "That might be a good idea."

Mrs. Cummings pinched the excess waist between her thumb and forefinger and closed the safety pin. She stepped back to get a better look. She, Bertram, and Mr. Cummings were all standing in front of the big hall mirror, attention focused on the slacks.

"Well," Bertram's mother said, "that's about the best I can do."

Bertram looked at himself closely, thinking hard of the pictures he'd seen in one of his father's old issues of *Esquire*. He had found it last night while rummaging through the basement and had been struck by the words on the cover: THIS FALL, THE CASUAL LOOK FOR THE CASUAL GUY. The magazine was full of photos of men standing around in leaf piles, looking at their watches. Bertram had noticed right off that there were two things that made these guys look casual. One was that they all wore bright, baggy pants that seemed to be too big for them, the other was that they all had sweaters tied around their necks.

"I think they should stay up if you try not to—to move too fast," Mrs. Cummings said.

Bertram nodded and walked over to a chair to pick up a dark green sweater that was lying on it.

"You're sure you wouldn't rather wear a pair of your own pants?" Mr. Cummings said.

"Positive, Dad." Bertram draped the sweater over his shoulders, tied it at the sleeves, and examined himself in the mirror. *This* is the look, he thought. The green sweater tied around his neck, the yellow alligator shirt, the checked golfing pants (exactly like the ones in *Esquire*), and finally, the white shoes. Add to that his perfectly parted, perfectly flat hair—he had spent an hour wetting, spraying, and combing it—and here he was, the ultimate casual guy.

"Well," Bertram said, looking first at his mom, then at his dad, "what do you think?"

They were silent for a moment, looking at one another. Then Mr. Cummings said, "Well . . ." and Mrs. Cummings chimed, "You look awfully . . . bright, dear."

"Thanks, Mom," Bertram said. He leaned close and gave her a kiss on the cheek.

Mrs. Cummings sniffed. "Did you take a shower this morning, Bertram?"

Bertram grabbed the collar of his shirt and smelled. "That's just mothballs, Mom."

"Oh."

"See you, Dad," Bertram said, getting his books and heading for the door.

"Why don't I give you a ride to school, son?" Mr. Cummings suggested. "I'm going that way anyway."

"No, thanks," Bertram said. "I want everybody to get a look at what I'm wearing today. Bye." Bertram gave a jaunty wave and stepped out into the beautiful October morning.

He arrived at his locker at precisely two minutes to eight. Just as he had thought, his new casual look had attracted a ton of shocked stares and whispers. From the moment he entered the school, students and teachers alike stopped in midstep, looked up, blinked, and either shook their heads or said something to someone standing close by.

They never thought it was possible, Bertram thought as he spun the dial. They never thought I could suddenly pull it all together and become . . . a man of style.

"Hey, Cummings," some guy from across the hall shouted, "throw a bucket of water on yourself, quick!"

Bertram turned and saw that the guy was Art Kinney and he was laughing as if what he'd just said was hysterically funny. Bertram shook his head, pitying the poor oaf, dressed in his T-shirt, jeans, and sneakers.

"Oh, boy," Bertram heard from behind him, close by. He recognized the voice, turned around, and saw Dalton standing and staring.

Bertram grinned.

"Oh, boy," Dalton said again.

"I took your advice and it's really paid off," Bertram said, retying the sleeves of his sweater.

"My advice?"

"Casual. Casual with style."

"But Bertram, I—"

"It took me a while to figure out what you really meant by it, but I finally found it." He took a step back and turned around once. "See?"

Dalton nodded. "I see."

Bertram looked at his watch. "It's eight o'clock. Now-or-never time." He got the last of his books from his locker. From one of the books, he pulled out the letter from Louise, brought it up close to his nose, closed his eyes, and took a sniff. He held it for a moment, thinking of her and letting the sweet smell swim around in his nostrils. Then he slid the letter back into the book.

"What about the glasses?" Bertram asked.

"What about them?" Dalton said.

Bertram slipped them off. The world around him suddenly became pea soup. He blinked and tried hard to focus on something.

"How many fingers am I holding up?" Dalton said.

"Three," Bertram guessed.

"Nice try. My hands are in my pockets."

"Someday I'm going to get contact lenses," Bertram said, putting on his glasses and bringing the world back into focus. It would be part of his new image— no more dumpy clothes, no more glasses, no more nerd.

"Well," Bertram said, as he prepared to start off toward Louise's locker.

"Well," Dalton said. "Good luck."

Bertram grinned, hoping it was a dashing grin. "I don't need luck. I've got style."

Dalton nodded. "Like I said—good luck."

As if on cue, the eight o'clock bell rang, signaling the students that classes began in fifteen minutes. Bertram joined the flow of kids and rounded the corner. Ten feet in front of him was the locker marked L. Baker. And standing before that locker was *her.*

Her with the fine, fair skin, the shimmering blond hair, the graceful dancer's walk. Her with the emerald eyes and the tiny bent nose and the clear, even smile.

Bertram sighed.

Louise Baker yawned.

For as long as she could remember, she had always hated the morning. Getting up was a trial for her, a test of will and strength. Most people fought the urge to go back to bed for the first five minutes or so; Louise fought it for a good two hours. If she got up at seven thirty, she walked around in a semidaze until nine thirty or ten, smiling and nodding, but understanding very little. Her mother told her it was just the way her inner clock was wound. Everyone (her mother claimed) had his or her own inner clock, and Louise's own clock didn't get her going until nine thirty or ten. Louise supposed that was as good an explanation as any. But right now explanations meant very little to her. Right now the only things that would have meant anything to her were a quiet room, a soft bed, warm blankets.

Louise Baker yawned again.

As always, she had to fight to remember what her first class was. History? Science? Algebra? That first class was always such a daze anyway. Then it hit her: economic geography.

It was while she was poking around in the top shelf of her locker for her economic geography book that she felt someone standing close by—someone looking at her.

She spun her head around and suddenly had to squint. If there was one thing she couldn't stand in the morning it was loud colors. They startled her the same way bright sunlight did, or a sudden sharp sound. They threatened to jangle her out of her daze.

And these colors were so loud—screaming yellows, howling greens, barking plaids—that she wasn't even able to make out who it was she was looking at. For Louise, it was like trying to look at someone standing in front of a spotlight.

"Hello, Louise," the colorful person said.

Louise took a small step back and tilted her head to one side. The *face* was familiar, but she was positive she'd never seen hair like that before: so heavily wetted and so tightly plastered down that it looked like a helmet.

"Hello—" Louise began, still trying to get a good look at the face as her eyes adjusted. Then all at once it came to her—those glasses, that voice, it must be . . . "Bertram?"

A smile broke across his face.

It was him. That boy from her science class, the brainy one who stuttered when he talked to her. Could this really be the same person?

"Bertram," she said. "You've changed."

"Yes," he replied, then reached into one of his books and pulled out a purple envelope. "And, well, here I am." He waved the envelope under his chin like a fan.

"Yes. . . . Here you are." The smell suddenly hit her and she felt as if she'd just been run over by a truck full of dead roses.

"Don't be nervous," Bertram said, still waving the envelope, then taking a whiff. "It's perfectly all right. I understand."

"Yes," Louise said, choking down a cough, "but I'm not sure *I* do." Why was he waving that envelope like that? Was this some kind of joke? Or was he really trying to make her sick with the smell?

"This"—Bertram waved the envelope in a circle—"told me everything I need to know."

Louise couldn't help but wave the oncoming smell away with her hand. She knew it was impolite, but then so was the scent of the envelope.

And then she was suddenly aware of being watched again. She looked down the hall and saw Mike Godey and his friends Chuck and Dennis crouched behind the water fountain.

And they were laughing. No, not just laughing. They were dying. They were looking at Bertram and Louise and pointing and their faces were bright red and they literally could not get their breath. Their laughter was getting louder and for a moment Louise wondered whether she was dreaming this, it was all so weird. Bertram dressed the way he was and the smell of that letter and these three jerks laughing their heads off.

Bertram suddenly noticed them and he looked surprised and Louise knew that this must be some kind of joke.

And Mike and his buddies stood up and came over and circled around Bertram and they were laughing so joyously that Louise couldn't help but join in. It still didn't make much sense, and maybe the joke was on *her*, but she had to admit something was funny.

" 'Dearest Bertram,' " Mike said in a high, mocking voice. " 'I'm really sorry about today in the library. For weeks now—' " But he couldn't finish the sentence, he couldn't even get a breath, he was collapsing from the inside with hysterical laughter.

But Bertram wasn't. Louise saw that; Bertram wasn't even smiling. In fact he looked like he was about to—

" 'For weeks now,' " Dennis chimed in in the same high voice, " 'I've been waiting for you to come and talk to me and then that stupid Mike Godey—' "

When Bertram heard that, he gave Dennis a shove and started to run. He got about two feet, before Chuck slammed into him and sent him sprawling into the lockers, and suddenly Louise knew something was going on. Mike and Bertram had never liked one another, she knew that, and Mike probably hated Bertram for what he'd done to him yesterday in science class, but what was going on? What was this all about?

Bertram stumbled to his feet and got past the three guys, mainly because they were so wiped out from laughing. But a small crowd had formed now and Bertram had to shove and push to get through them and then Louise saw something at the waist of his pants coming undone—it looked like a safety pin—and all at once the pants were dropping and this was just too much for eight o'clock in the morning. She knew that whatever was happening, Bertram was embarrassed and angry, but she just couldn't help it.

She kept on laughing.

And so did everyone else in the crowd, which seemed to grow bigger and bigger by the second.

Bertram got to his pants just as they came down around his knees, revealing a pair of polka-dot boxer shorts, but just as he was pulling them up the sweater around his neck came undone, so he had to grab that, which of course meant that his pants fell back down, which of course meant that the laughter of the crowd became deafening and so did the comments:

"—I don't believe this!—"

"—only Bertram!—"

"—what a nerd!—"

"—somebody get him some suspenders!—"

"—somebody get him a robe!—"

Bertram finally managed to pull everything up and together, finally managed to get firmly on his feet, finally managed to tear through the crowd and go running down the hall.

And finally, Louise stopped laughing, thinking that maybe this hadn't been so funny after all. A lot of things she wouldn't have normally found funny got her laughing in the morning, and immediately she was sorry she had laughed, sorry she hadn't stepped in and helped Bertram.

But it was too late now.

Dalton caught sight of Bertram just outside the library. He was half running, half hopping, holding the front of his pants with one hand and his green sweater with the other. This clued Dalton to one fact fast: it hadn't gone well with Louise.

"Bertram!" Dalton yelled. He ran over to him. "Bertram, wh—?"

Bertram's eyes were glazed, his face stony. He was staring straight ahead.

"That was *it,*" he said quietly, intently.

"What happened?"

Bertram turned at the door to the library. Dalton followed him in.

"That was the last straw, the last straw that broke the last camel's back!" He was shouting now as he stalked across the library, heading for the less crowded stacks.

A librarian looked up and brought her finger to her lips. "Sssssh!"

"Oh, 'sshhh!' yourself!" Bertram snapped, and Dalton saw the poor old librarian's mouth drop open.

Luckily, before the old woman could snatch Bertram by the collar and haul him down to the principal's office, they had ascended the stairs to the stacks and were weaving between shelves of books.

Bertram tore off the green sweater and flung it into the air. It caught on one of the fluorescent lights and hung there.

"I've had it with being the fool," Bertram said, "the nerd everyone laughs at, the dupe of every joke. I've had it with people who think they can walk all over me!"

As Bertram walked around in circles, Dalton asked him what had happened.

"It was Godey! Godey wrote the letter and put the perfume all over it!"

"Well—" Dalton began, trying to think of some consoling words.

"But that wasn't the worst part," Bertram said, peeling off the Lacoste shirt, then drying his hair with it. *"She* was in on it!"

"Louise?"

"You bet Louise! She was in on the whole thing."

"How do you know?"

" 'Cause she stood there the whole time, laughing! She laughed at me, Dalton. I'm taking this stupid costume off and going home!"

"Bertram, hold it. We're in a library."

Bertram stopped and looked down at himself. He quickly wiggled back into his shirt. "They think they know about revenge? About humiliation? Lemme tell you, I wrote the book on humiliation, and I'm gonna start teaching some classes around here. Nobody makes a fool out of Bertram Cummings!" He then turned and marched off toward the back exit of the library.

Dalton didn't follow him. Instead, he reached up to the fluorescent light and took the sweater down. He wondered whether or not Bertram would want it back. Probably not. Bertram would probably go home, put all the clothes from the basement in a great big pile, and burn them. And then maybe he could forget all about it;

maybe he could forgive Louise and tolerate Godey and just let things settle down.

Maybe he could, but Dalton knew he wouldn't. Bertram wasn't going to forgive, forget, or tolerate. He was going to get even.

7

It had been over a week since the setup, and Mike and Bertram had not spoken a word to one another. This was fine with Mike. It kept things tense. Mike knew why *he* wasn't saying anything. He was waiting. Waiting for just the right moment to strike his final blow. As for why Bertram wasn't talking, well, that was pretty obvious. Every time he walked into a class—especially the science class—people were laughing behind his back, pointing, and saying "Did you hear? Did you hear what happened?" Mike ate it up. It was maybe the best revenge setup he'd ever pulled.

And it wasn't over yet.

The bell rang and everyone shuffled to their seats and sat down. Mike looked over at Bertram, who was slumped down low, his face behind a book. That's right, Mike thought, stay just like that, that's how I want to remember you.

Mr. Barnes strode in and went to his desk. He picked up a book, opened it, and started to read out loud.

Mike's hand shot up. He waved.

Barnes looked up over his glasses and stopped reading. "Yes, Mike?"

Mike knew Barnes couldn't stand him. Barnes liked his classes to run swiftly, precisely, with a minimum of fuss, like a chemistry experiment. But Mike fussed; he caused trouble, mouthed off, and wasn't afraid to speak his mind. Especially now.

"I've been thinking about that flying saucer I saw," he said.

"Mike, I think we've covered that territory pretty—"

Mike cut him off. "Yeah, well, I've been thinking and I've decided I didn't see a spotlight from Don's Used Car Lot. I've decided that what I saw was a flying saucer. From another planet."

Mike looked over at Bertram. He was still behind his book, not moving, barely even breathing.

The class was quiet.

Barnes was also looking at Bertram, and his eyebrows crinkled when he saw that Bertram wasn't jumping to his own defense.

"Uh, Bertram," Barnes finally said, "do you have anything to say about this?"

Bertram lowered his book and looked at Barnes. "No," he said.

"You don't?" Barnes asked.

Bertram shook his head.

Mike almost felt a chuckle escape, but he choked it down and managed to keep a straight face.

"Well, Mike," Barnes said, "so you've decided for yourself that it was a flying saucer."

"That's right," Mike said. "And what I want is for Bertram to apologize for what he said to me."

"Now, Mike—"

"I'm sorry," Bertram said, very quickly, very quietly, and not looking at Mike.

"What was that?" Mike said. "I didn't quite hear that."

Louder, but without looking at him, Bertram said, "I'm sorry."

"Thanks," Mike said. And then to Barnes: "Sorry for interrupting. Just wanted to clear this up."

Barnes paused a bit, nodded, and went back to reading from the text.

It was now two weeks later and Mike was still feeling pretty good. Things really seemed to be going his way lately. When he'd first switched from junior high to high school, all he could think about was how awful it was to be back on the bottom again, the way he was in first grade, or when he went from grade school to junior high. And it had been tough, those first few months, no doubt about it. After all, how could you possibly hope to be the coolest guy in school when there were so many guys around you who could actually drive a car? Or buy a drink in a bar? Or vote? In other words, Mike knew that as an entering freshman, he was nothing; no, worse than that, he was subnothing.

And it might have stayed that way for the rest of the year. Except for the prank.

Word had spread quickly, and three weeks later, some people were still talking about it. Seniors and juniors would come up to Mike and ask him how he did it. And Mike would take his time telling them about it. And when he was finished telling them about it, the seniors and juniors would smile, give him the thumbs-up sign, and say "All right."

After the last bell of the day had rung, Mike bolted

right from class to the front doors of the school. He didn't bother stopping off at his locker, since he didn't feel like doing any homework that night.

He ran the whole way home, and once there, bolted straight up the stairs to his room.

It was two hours before his parents got home, and that meant two hours that he could watch television in peace without his mom screaming for him to take out the garbage or his dad asking him how he did on his English test. He remembered there was a movie on he'd really wanted to see—*Ten Hands of Death,* on cable. One of the best kung fu movies ever made.

Mike threw himself down in front of the TV set, picked up the remote control, hit the ON button, and dialed the all-movie channel.

Ten Hands of Death was just starting. Two guys in red pajamas were kicking each other bloody. Mike had seen this part of the movie before. Just as one of the guys is starting to lose, he yanks his hand off and you find out that it was a fake hand all along, that his whole arm is really a sword.

Mike grinned when the guy with the sword arm started cutting the guy without the sword arm, because he knew the guy without the sword arm had poison darts hidden under his fingernails and—

Suddenly the picture flickered and the sound warbled. Mike shot up off the bed. He reached for the remote control.

The picture continued to flicker and then the sound died completely because some kind of static was coming in and the static started to get really loud. The picture began to get fuzzy and then disappeared.

Mike was scared. He didn't know why, but he was suddenly very frightened.

Because the TV wasn't dying, and it wasn't bad reception.

Another picture was forming.

It was a man.

Sort of.

As it started to become more and more clear, and as the static started to fade out, Mike began to get more and more scared.

The man was green, for starters. Mike was positive he was green, because he adjusted the color tuner on the remote control every which way and no matter what, the guy came up green.

Green and bald with enormous yellow eyes like a cat and some kind of a hose around his neck and no mouth.

The green bald guy had no mouth.

The picture finally established itself. The green guy was standing in front of some kind of panel that glowed yellow.

Almost without thinking, Mike hit the channel change button. It didn't make any difference. No matter what channel Mike went to, there was the bald green guy, staring at him.

Then the bald green guy did something that made Mike stop changing channels. He said, "Mich-ael Go-dey."

Mike shook his head to make sure he wasn't imagining all this.

The bald green guy repeated, "Mich-ael Go-dey."

He talked slowly and there was a funny warble to his voice, as if maybe he had two throats.

"Greetings, Michael Godey."

Mike couldn't think of much to say. He didn't even know if this guy could hear him. But just to be on the safe side he said, "Hi."

"I am Non of Zenka."

"Sure ya are." If I looked like him, I'd have a name like that, Mike thought.

"Unfortunately, we do not have two-way communication. I cannot see or hear you." Non of Zenka raised his right hand. He had two fat fingers—it looked almost like a paw—and there was no thumb.

I'm losing my mind, Mike thought. I'm imagining seeing a green bald guy talking to me from the TV, and he's got no thumbs.

"My message is urgent," Non continued. "Repeat, my message is urgent."

Mike looked over to see if his bedroom door was shut. It wasn't, so he got up quickly and closed it. If this was really happening, he wanted it to be his secret, and if he was going nuts, he wanted *that* to be a secret too.

"We are . . ." Non was saying, but a wave of static washed out the rest of his sentence. ". . . must contact . . . believers . . ." More static, and the picture started to go. ". . . fading . . . will . . . contact you later . . ."

The image faded out completely. Then, after a moment, *Ten Hands of Death* came back on.

Mike didn't even notice. His head was spinning with what had just happened. How long had it taken? Thirty seconds? A minute? And had it really happened? Mike looked around him—at his bed, his shelves, his desk, his window, his curtains. Everything now was just as it had been before. He wasn't losing his mind. Someone or something had just contacted him. Something with the power to jam his television. Something bald, and green, with no thumbs, something—

—from another planet?

Mike smiled at the thought, because if it was true, if it

had really happened and if he or she or it was from another planet, one thing was for sure.

It was contacting Mike Godey. And Mike Godey alone.

The room was dark and quiet, the only light being the gentle glow of the plastic wall panel behind him, the only sound being that of the tiny desk computer as it whirred and buzzed softly.

Bertram reached up and pulled the green plastic head off. He shook his hair, which was sticky with sweat, then ran his hand through it. He slipped off the glove and scratched his head. Boy, did it get hot under that helmet. He wondered for a moment if he couldn't cool it down by opening up the back or maybe getting an air hose in there.

But then again, it didn't really matter. If everything went as planned, he'd only have to wear this costume a few more times.

Bertram walked over to the camera and switched it off. He shut down the computer and the monitor. But before he did this, he took one last look at Mike Godey's house. Just what was Godey thinking right now? Just what was going through that little pebble brain of his?

"Bertram!" his mother called again.

Bertram got up and crossed quickly to the door to make sure it was locked. "Yeah, Mom?"

"Have you seen the vacuum cleaner? I've been looking all over for it!"

Bertram looked down at his alien body: the tubes running up from his back into his chest, the strange suctionlike configurations on his shoulders, and the bristle brush protrusions on his arms. Then he looked at the remains of the vacuum cleaner sitting on his bed, resembling more than anything else a giant electronic turkey the day after Thanksgiving.

"Uh, no, Mom," Bertram called back, "I haven't!"

8

Bertram tipped his head a little closer to the bookshelf. The conversation was hard to hear. Mike, Dennis, and Chuck were speaking in whispers.

"I wasn't dreaming!" Mike hissed.

"Maybe it was some kind of interference," Dennis said.

"Yeah, interference," Chuck said.

"Interference doesn't talk to you," Mike shot back.

Bertram pulled his head back and looked up and down the library aisle, looking for a better position from which to hear. One of the shelves near the bottom was clear of books, and as Bertram bent down, he could see their feet and heard "Maybe it was another TV show."

"Another TV show doesn't have a bald green guy look at you and say your name."

"A bald green guy?" Chuck said. "Must have been an educational show."

Bertram heard Mike let out an exasperated sigh. "I

am tellin' you guys that some alien is trying to get in contact with us."

A pause. Then Dennis said, "Why'd he pick you?"

"Hey, if you were an alien, wouldn't *you* want to contact the coolest guy in school?"

It was all Bertram could do to keep from exploding with laughter. Between the three of them, they didn't have one brain in working order. He couldn't stand to listen to any more. He just had to know that the ball had begun rolling in the right direction, and everything was set for tonight. So he pulled his head out of the shelf, got up on his hands and knees, and began crawling toward the stairs.

At around the L's of DRAMA he ran into a pair of brown loafers, and heard "Bertram?"

Bertram straightened up and found himself kneeling in front of Mr. Barnes.

"Oh, hi, Mr. Barnes."

"You looking for something?"

"Uhh . . . uhh . . . yeah. And I found it."

Mr. Barnes nodded. "Need a hand up?" He held his out.

Bertram took it and pulled himself up to his feet. "Thanks."

They both headed for the stairs. On the way they passed Mike and company, still huddled together in the stacks. Bertram couldn't help but smile slyly when he saw them.

"How's the experiment coming?" Mr. Barnes asked, as they went down the stairs.

"Oh, fine. Fine."

"You've licked that frequency-honing problem, then?"

"Oh, yeah." Bertram nodded vigorously.

"I hope you'll be ready to demonstrate it soon. I'm looking forward to it."

"You won't be disappointed, sir."

"I've been meaning to ask you—is everything all right?"

"Sir?"

"You've been very quiet in class. Quieter than usual. Is there . . . anything you'd like to talk about?"

Bertram hesitated before answering. He couldn't take the chance—if Barnes were to get a whiff of what was going on between him and Mike, it could jeopardize everything.

"No, sir," Bertram said. "I'll try to contribute more in class, though."

"I don't want to force you."

"No, it wouldn't be forcing me. I have a few things I'd like to get off my chest."

Barnes nodded. They had reached the hall doors. "I'll see you in class then."

"See you there," Bertram said. He watched Barnes stride out of the library and down the hall. A bit of guilt twanged somewhere inside him. He knew that what he was doing wasn't exactly *wrong*—no one was going to be permanently hurt—but he also knew that if he told Mr. Barnes about it, or if Barnes were to hear of it, he would frown on the whole idea and say something like "Bertram, you're a *scientist*, and scientists must be responsible, must raise themselves above the petty jealousies of everyday life."

"Hey, Bertram!"

Bertram's daydream of Barnes vanished like a soap bubble. Dalton was walking over to him.

"Where you been all hour?" he asked. "I looked, you weren't around."

"I was up in the stacks," Bertram said.

"Research?"

"Something like that."

"Hey, what are you doing after school today?"

Bertram thought a moment. Was this the right time to bring Dalton in?

"You're not busy again? I've hardly seen you in the last three weeks. You've been going right home after school, you don't want to talk on the phone . . ."

"Well, I *am* kind of busy," Bertram said, then added, "But why don't you come over after school and I'll show you what I've been up to."

"Okay," Dalton said. "Four o'clock?"

"Fine."

At four forty-five Dalton was sitting on Bertram's bed, watching him tinker.

Dalton was beginning to worry about his friend. Ever since Mike had pulled that stupid stunt, Bertram had been like a zombie. He was always scratching some ideas into a notebook, or mumbling to himself, or biting his lip and staring off into space. After school he went right home, and whenever Dalton tried to phone or stop by, he was told by Bertram's mother or father that their son "didn't wish to be disturbed."

Something was definitely up.

"Have you talked to Louise?" Dalton asked, more to kill the dead silence than anything else.

"Not exactly," Bertram mumbled.

"What do you mean not exactly? Either you have or you haven't."

"Well, I haven't yet. But I will soon. Sort of." And then Bertram chuckled, as if he'd just made some small joke.

Dalton started to say something, but the computer in front of Bertram suddenly hummed to life. The monitor blinked on, showing a grid map of the houses in the neighborhood. Bertram touched a button. Four of the houses glowed bright red. Dalton got up off the bed and moved over next to his friend.

Bertram hit a few buttons, then adjusted the dish antenna with a screwdriver. This done, he stood up and walked over to a darkened corner of the room and pulled out the camera, sitting on its tripod. He fiddled with that, then walked over to a far wall, where a white sheet hung. He pulled the sheet down, revealing a large plastic wall panel. Bertram hit a switch and the panel lit up, casting a strange, throbbing glow on the room.

"Bertram," Dalton said slowly, "whose houses are these?"

"One is Mike's, the other is Dennis's, another is Chuck's, and another is . . . Louise's."

"So this is it."

"What?"

"Your revenge."

Bertram said nothing. He fiddled with the camera.

Dalton went on, "Your revenge is to interrupt their favorite afternoon TV shows."

Bertram smiled and made that same, small chuckling sound.

"Something like that," he said quietly. "Do me a favor—hand me that alien head on the shelf."

Alien head?

Dalton looked, and there it was. Green and bowl-shaped, with enormous eyes and sort of a speaker box where the mouth should have been. He picked it up—it was surprisingly light—and turned it around in his hands.

It was a fishbowl, spraypainted green; the eyes were 150-watt light bulbs, painted yellow; the speaker box was something pulled off the front of an old TV set.

Dalton turned around to hand the head to Bertram and saw that he had slipped on a costume to match the head. He was wearing a tight-fitting green shirt (long underwear, dyed) and a sort of bluish doublet over his chest (a ski vest worn backwards). Hanging all over the shirt and vest were all kinds of mechanical parts and blinking lights. Two big hoses came up from the back around the neck and met at the chest.

Silently, Dalton gave Bertram the head, and noticed that he had on large, two-fingered gloves (a pair of mittens, cut down the middle and sewn into two parts, with the thumbs removed).

Bertram took the head and slipped it on. He flipped a switch on the front of his chest, then spoke in a voice that made him sound like he was underwater.

"Gr-eet-ings," Bertram the Alien said.

"I don't get it," Dalton said.

"You will," Bertram said as he stepped over between the plastic wall panel and the camera. "Do me a favor. Hit the BROADCAST button on the panel there."

Dalton hit it. The dish antenna made a whirring noise, then swung left. The red houses on the computer monitor suddenly went yellow, then green.

A red light on top of the camera popped on. And Bertram the Alien raised his right paw in greeting.

On his way home from school that day Mike had stopped at The Book Company and picked up a copy of *U.F.O.'s and You*. He was engrossed in the third chapter, which dealt with space kidnapings, when his television picture started to flicker and flip.

Mike looked up, startled but also relieved. He hadn't dreamed it after all, because here it was again, this time interrupting an episode of *Starsky and Hutch*.

"Greetings from Zenka," came the warbly voice, followed immediately by the image of the green head. "I am contacting . . . Michael Godey."

Mike set the book down and bounced over to the end of the bed.

The alien went on. "I am also contacting Charles Benson."

Oh, my god, Mike thought. He's contacting Chuck.

Chuck Benson was leaning against the sink, washing the breakfast dishes that had been soaking all day and watching *The Alamo,* a western. It was right at the part of the movie when all the Mexicans start busting into the Alamo that the picture started to go, and then the sound.

A few seconds later a green guy with huge yellow eyes came on, looked at Chuck, and said his name.

Chuck dropped a cup.

The guy with the yellow eyes continued. "I am also contacting Dennis Kutchinson."

Dennis Kutchinson was sprawled out in his bed, half asleep from having read the first chapter of *Idylls of the King*. The TV was on and was tuned to an afternoon talk show called *Kids' Problems*. Two ten-year-olds were being interviewed and were talking about how much they hated to take out the garbage, when the screen fizzed and the sound fuzzed and Dennis, his eyes blinking open, heard a weird voice say his name.

He sat up and stared into two yellow eyes that stared

right back. He couldn't think of anything to say, so he hiccupped, which he usually did when he was startled.

The guy on the TV set said, "And I am contacting—"

Mrs. Baker was sitting in front of the television set in the living room watching the evening news and folding some freshly done laundry. Her husband walked into the room and crossed over to the set. As he bent down to adjust the color, the picture suddenly jumped, the sound crackled, and a green man with no hair and no thumbs stared out and said, "I am contacting . . . Louise Baker."

Mr. Baker straightened up and looked at his wife.

Mrs. Baker folded a pair of boxer shorts and called; "Louise! Television for you!"

Mr. Baker took a step back, then sat down next to his wife as Louise came bounding down the stairs. She ran into the room, a quizzical look on her face, and said, "Mom, did you—?" And then she caught sight of the set, and the whatever-it-was who had asked to speak to her.

"I am Non of Zenka," it said. "I am from the Andromeda galaxy. I am an emissary to Earth."

Louise said nothing, sat down, and like Mike, Chuck, and Dennis in their houses, watched and listened attentively.

"I require your obedience and assistance in telling the people of Earth of my arrival. In order so that there will be as little confusion as possible, we would like to begin by telling the *young* people of your world of our arrival."

Bertram paused slightly and Dalton had to marvel at the daring of it all, the sheer ingenuity.

"We come in peace," Bertram warbled from behind the mask. "We require your assistance. We will contact you tomorrow about the details . . . same time . . . any channel." Bertram pointed at Dalton. Dalton hit the BROADCAST OFF button, and all the various lights of the system shut down.

After a moment Bertram reached up and pulled the grotesque green head off. He breathed a heavy sigh. Then he looked at Dalton and grinned.

"Well?" he said.

"Well, Mike *is* pretty dumb, but do you really think he's that dumb?"

"Hook, line, and sinker."

"And Louise?"

Bertram walked over to the workbench. "She'll have her doubts at first, but she'll eventually go for it. Help me off with this thing." Dalton grabbed onto the shoulders of the vest and pulled it over Bertram's head.

"And then what?" Dalton asked.

"And then," Bertram replied, "they're all going to be very sorry they ever messed with Bertram Cummings."

9

Louise Baker had her doubts.

As soon as the bald green man who said he was Non of Zenka from the Andromeda galaxy got off the TV, Louise went into the family room, picked up the phone, and called Mike Godey.

"Hello?" Mike answered.

"This is Louise Baker," Louise said.

"I know. I heard you were contacted too!"

"Contacted? All I know is, this green guy came on and started talking about a lot of stuff I don't understand."

"He's an alien, don't you see? And he's coming to Earth. . . ."

"Look, are you and your dumb friends playing a trick on me?"

"Are you kidding?" Mike exploded. "This is the second time I've been contacted. This is the real thing. You, me, Chuck, Dennis. We've been picked to help the alien greet Earth."

Louise thought about it all for a moment. It didn't

make very much sense. Why would somebody from another planet contact a bunch of high school freshmen? You'd at least think he'd contact seniors, or people in college.

"Well," Louise said slowly, "I'm sure it'll be fun, but I'm busy right now."

"Louise, listen to me. It's obvious he's picked us all very carefully, that he knows all about us, that he sees us as a *team*. He thinks we each have special abilities—obviously, he wants me for my cool and my brains—"

Oh, boy, Louise thought, rolling her eyes.

"—and Chuck and Dennis for their . . . for their . . . you know, loyalty. And you, because everybody trusts you. And you're so likable and wholesome and everything."

This is just too much, she thought.

"Don't you understand?" Mike said. "We'll make history. Nobody has ever been able to prove they've been contacted by an alien. I've been reading all about it in this book. Do you realize how rich we'll be? How famous?"

That part, she had to admit, made some sense. If the alien was real, it sure would be something if she could say he called her first. And if the rich and famous part was true, she could afford twice as many dance lessons—who could tell? Maybe she could even start her own dance school.

"You sure this isn't some kind of trick?" she asked, warily.

"Cross my heart," Mike said, and then for emphasis: "Cross my heart and hope to die choking on a nail."

"Okay," Louise said, making a face at the phone. "I believe you."

"Great. What we'll do, then, is meet at school in the

library. The stack section marked DRAMA. Know where it is?"

"Yes."

"And we'll make plans to go over to somebody's house and get the next transmission. Got it?"

"Got it."

"Okay. Well, it's great to have you aboard. This is going to be the most incredible, the most amazing, the most stupefyingly unbelievable—"

"I'll see you tomorrow, Mike," Louise said. "Bye."

"Okay. Bye."

Louise hung up, wondering what it was about most boys that made them such monkeys half the time. She shook her head and walked back up to her room.

Mike Godey felt like he was flying. As he walked through the halls at school and looked at all the people around him, he absolutely *had* to feel superior. After all, he knew things now that they'd never dreamed were true or possible. He knew things that people a hundred years from now would look back on and compare to the discovery of America, the signing of the Declaration of Independence, and the first flight of man.

In all the history books Mike Godey would be side by side with Columbus, Thomas Jefferson, Einstein, Lincoln, the Wright brothers, and Thomas Edison. The name Mike Godey would be on the lips of school kids for years to come; they would have to memorize his name along with all the important dates of his life; they would be *tested* on it.

That thought delighted Mike. All the kids, just like the ones he was looking at now, grumbling and complaining and sweating because they were being tested on the life of Mike Godey, the first earthling ever to be contacted by an alien being.

So wrapped up was he in dreams of his own greatness that he didn't see the kid coming around the corner who bumped his shoulder and sent his books flying.

Mike whirled around, then smiled. He had bumped right into the person he most wanted to bump into that day.

Bertram Cummings.

"Woops," Bertram said, blandly. "Sorry, Mike."

Mike bent down and scooped the books up. "You better look where you're going from now on, Cummings."

"Oh, gee, I will, Mike," Bertram said with just an edge of sarcasm.

"And you'd *better* watch the way you talk to me."

Bertram just looked bored, and turned away slightly.

"You know why?" Mike said, loudly. "You know why you'd better watch it, Cummings?" A small crowd was gathering. Good, Mike thought. He wanted everybody to hear this. It would give them all a taste of what was to come. "Because I believe that there are aliens, and real soon I am gonna have proof. Boy, am I gonna have proof!"

Bertram's eyebrows rose up over his glasses. "Proof that there are really aliens?"

"You bet."

"How? Your relatives coming for a visit?"

The small crowd laughed, then looked to Mike. The ball was in his court. But he couldn't think of a comeback. Not just yet.

"Funny, Cummings," Mike snapped. "But you'll see."

Bertram nodded, smiled, turned, and walked on down the hall.

Maybe, Mike thought, if the aliens from Zenka need slave labor for some far-off planet outpost, he could recommend Bertram. Mike grinned at the thought. When Non and his people came, that would be the first thing to bring up.

Seated once again between the glowing plastic panel and the camera, Bertram adjusted his alien head so he could see a little better.

"Dalton, could you move to the right a little?"

"Like this?" Dalton said.

"Yeah. And could you hold the cards up a little higher?"

Dalton lifted the enormous cue cards till his face was almost completely hidden by them. "Like this?"

"Great. What time is it?"

"Five exactly."

"Okay," Bertram said, then cleared his throat. "Hit the button." Inside his plastic fishbowl head, Bertram could hear all the intricate broadcast mechanisms click into place. He tilted his head down a little so he could see the top of the camera. As soon as the red light went on, he began reading off the cue cards in front of him. "I am contacting Louise Baker, Charles Benson, Dennis Kutchinson, and Michael Godey."

Bertram paused as Dalton flipped to the next card.

"We of Zenka wish to contact a governing body of young people. We require a public gathering to broadcast our message."

Dalton flipped the card.

"Our researchers tell us that the governing board of you young people is known as . . . the student council.

You must set up a receiver at the meeting of this student council."

The next card that came up was upside down. Bertram was unable to read it, and couldn't remember what he was supposed to say next.

"Uuuhhh." He waved a hand, trying to signal Dalton. But Dalton couldn't see him over the cards. "Uuuhh, one moment, please, there is some subspace interference."

The card remained upside down.

"A *malfunction* . . . from the planet *Daltonus!*"

Dalton finally stuck his head up. Bertram pointed to the card. Dalton saw the mistake and turned the card over.

"Ahh," Bertram said. "All is well now. As I was saying . . . you must set up a receiver at the meeting of this student council. We plan to make contact on what you earthlings call Tuesday. . . . Our message is of the utmost importance, and your help will be rewarded. I, Non of Zenka, thank you. Farewell, for now."

Dalton dropped the last card and reached over and hit the OFF button. The little red light went out. Bertram pulled off his head.

"Whew," he said, taking a breath. "It gets stuffy in here."

"I can't believe this is really working," Dalton said.

"Believe it. Not only did I hear Godey and his friends talking in the library, but I ran into him today in the hall. And he practically told me the flying saucers were on their way."

"And Louise?"

"I don't know for sure how she's taking it yet. But come Tuesday, I'll find out. Help me off with these gloves, will you?"

"Oh, boy," Dennis said, after Louise had shut the TV off.

"Oh, wow," said Chuck.

"I didn't really believe it last night," Dennis said.

"Me neither," Chuck said.

"But I do now."

"Me too."

"Boy."

"Wow."

Louise returned to her chair. They were all sitting in her family room.

"I wonder how that alien knows the student council meets on Tuesdays," said Dennis.

Mike, sitting on the couch, rolled his eyes. "He's a higher life form, Dennis. He probably even knows what room they meet in. Use your head, okay?"

"Okay, you don't have to get so mad!"

"Well, you don't have to act like such a dork!"

"I'm not a dork!"

"Oh, you are too a dork!"

Now Louise rolled her eyes. If Non really was a higher life form, why on earth did he pick these three?

"Enough," Louise said firmly. "We have a lot of work to do. And not much time."

"What kind of work?" Chuck said.

"Well, the student council isn't just going to turn their meeting over to us on Tuesday. And we aren't just going to be able to go down to the AV room and pick up a video screen. This is all going to take planning. We're going to have to talk to the principal."

Dennis, Chuck, and Mike all groaned.

"She hates me," said Mike.

"Well, we'll never be able to do this without Mrs.

Mead's permission. We're just going to have to go into her office and tell her . . ." Louise bit her lip, thinking. "Tell her we've got something special to show the school, something we can't really explain."

"She'll never buy that," Mike said.

"No way," Dennis concurred. "She doesn't really trust kids."

"I don't think she even *likes* kids," Chuck said.

"I guess I'll be doing the talking," Louise said. "But we all have to go in together."

"Well, you're right, I guess," Mike said, getting up to go. "But I'll tell *you* something—it'll be the first and last time I ever go to the principal's office willingly."

"Me too," from Dennis.

"Ditto," from Chuck.

"C'mon, guys, let's go over to my house." Mike headed for the door. "What time tomorrow, Louise?"

"Ten fifteen, between classes."

"Okay. See you then."

Louise opened the front door for them. "Good night." The three of them all walked through, each crowding the other to be the first one out.

"Watch it!"

"Don't tell me—*you* watch it!"

"Well, you'd better watch it from now on!"

"Oh, yeah?"

"Yeah."

"Yeah yourself!"

Louise closed the door. The sound of their barking voices faded and she was left alone to contemplate the meeting with the formidable Mrs. Mead.

10

The four of them were seated in a semicircle in front of Mrs. Mead's big metal desk. Mrs. Mead, whom Louise had always thought was pretty in a tough kind of way, sat with her hands folded on the desk, her thumbs pressed up in a pyramid.

"Well, what can I do for you?" she asked.

Louise said, "We want to get some time at the next student council meeting."

"Some time?" Mrs. Mead said. "What do you mean?"

"To make a presentation," Louise replied.

"What kind of presentation?"

Louise squirmed a little and looked over at Mike, sitting right next to her. "A video presentation."

"So you want to use the video screen."

"That's right." Louise smiled brightly, feeling relieved that it had all been so simple.

"And what is it you're going to present?"

Oh, no. Now what? Definitely not the truth. No matter what she told Mrs. Mead, it couldn't be the truth. "Well," Louise muttered, "we can't say, not just yet."

Mrs. Mead snapped a hard glance at Mike. "Okay, Godey, what's up?"

Mike gave his best Who, Me? smile and said, "What do you mean, Mrs. Mead?"

"Don't snow me, Godey."

"Honest, Mrs. Mead," Louise cut in, "we really can't say."

"Why not?"

"Look," Mike said, leaning forward in his chair, "can I be perfectly honest with you?"

"You can try."

"The most amazing thing ever in the history of the world is happening right now."

"Don't tell me. You're passing English."

Mike laughed halfheartedly. "That's good. That's funny." He looked at Dennis and Chuck. "Right?"

"Right, Mike."

"Right. Ha, ha."

"Seriously, though," Mike continued, "it's really difficult to explain. But we need a video screen for the student council meeting. We have something very important to show."

Mrs. Mead shook her head and sat back in her chair. "Unless you can convince me of the sincerity and importance of your request, no deal."

Silence from everyone. Well, that's it, Louise thought. A no is a no.

Mike said, "Ma'am, the four of us have been contacted by a—"

And before Louise even had time to think about it, she shifted in her seat, brought her foot back, and kicked Mike squarely in the shin.

"OWWWWWW!"

This broke his train of thought long enough for Louise to say, "Mrs. Mead, we really don't have anything up our sleeves, or anyplace else. We have a presentation, and we want it to be a secret. It has to be a surprise."

Mike was holding his ankle, rubbing it. Mrs. Mead looked at him. "What's wrong?"

"Nothing," Mike said. "Old football injury."

"See," Louise went on, "we can't tell you about it because we . . . we promised somebody. And it's wrong to break a promise, isn't it?"

"Well . . ." Mrs. Mead hesitated. "It depends on the promise."

"Then I'll make a promise to *you*. All of us will. If this is some kind of practical joke, or anything that'll turn out to be embarrassing to anyone or waste the council's time, we'll all take detentions."

Mike, Chuck, and Dennis all looked at her, eyes wide. The word "detention" had put the fear of God Almighty into them.

Mrs. Mead said, "All right. It's a deal. The only thing that still worries me, though, is the equipment. None of you have any experience working with it, do you?"

All four shook their heads.

"Then I want someone to operate it who knows what they're doing. Someone like Brian Bauer or . . . Bertram Cummings. He's quite technically minded."

"Bertram!" Mike shouted. "No way! Forget it! We—"

Louise hauled back and connected savagely with Mike's other shin.

"OWWWWWWWWWW!"

She smiled sweetly. "Bertram will be fine, Mrs. Mead."

Bertram was doing math homework when the phone rang. He reached across his workbench and picked it up.

"Hello?"

"Bertram?"

Bertram felt his heart jump. He knew right away who it was.

"Yeah?"

"This is Louise."

Bertram cleared his throat. "Louise?" he said. "Louise Whom?"

"Louise *Baker.* From science."

"Oh. Oh, yeah. Hi. How are you?"

"I'm fine. How are you?"

"Fine."

Pause. Silence. His fear that she might be calling because she'd figured the whole thing out vanished. This was definitely something else.

"Bertram?"

"Still here."

"I'm calling to ask you a favor."

"Uh-huh."

"This coming Tuesday, during homeroom, during the student council meeting, are you free?"

Bertram had to think a moment, because he *wasn't* free. He was planning to be here, in his room. But he certainly couldn't tell her that. And anyway, the question had interesting consequences.

"I think so," he lied.

"It's just that we need your help with some video equipment."

" 'We?' "

"Me and, um, some friends of mine."

Smart girl, he thought, not mentioning Godey. "What kind of help do you need?"

"Oh, nothing really big. You know, just setting up that video screen, focusing . . . and that's about it. I really can't explain everything. It's kind of a secret."

"That's okay."

"You'll help out, then?"

"Sure. No problem." No problem at all.

"Oh, that's great. And you'll find out what the secret is tomorrow. I wish I could tell you now, but—"

"I understand."

"I knew you would. Okay, then. I'll see you tomorrow, right before homeroom, in the AV room."

"See you then," Bertram said coolly, hung up, then screamed with sheer joy. Perfect. Oh, God, it was so perfect, it was not to be believed. The irony, the wonderful, beautiful irony of it. He had to tell Dalton. . . .

"Hello?"

"Hello, Dalton?"

"Hey, Bertram. What's up?"

"You're never going to believe this."

"Try me."

"Guess who just called?"

"Florence Nightingale."

"Not even close. Louise Baker."

"What'd she want?"

"Are you sitting down?"

"Lying down."

"Good. You're in just the position to faint. She and her cohorts want me to run the video for them for the broadcast tomorrow." There was only quiet from Dalton's end. "Can you believe that? Can you?"

"This all sounds like it's going too far."

"Too far? Are you kidding? It couldn't be better. If I

had planned this part, it couldn't be better." He let a chuckle bubble up from his throat.

"You're going to get in a lot of trouble. You know that, don't you?"

"It's worth it."

"It's crazy, is what it is. This revenge thing has driven you over the brink."

"Listen, Dalton, they asked for this. It's too late to back out now."

"It's not too late. You could make a broadcast—say your spaceship broke down on Alpha Centauri and you won't be here till 1993."

"You think they'd believe that? No way. And you're nuts if you think I'm not going through with it. It's going to be the biggest day of my life."

"The biggest disaster, you mean."

"Well, you can be there to find out, along with everybody else."

"Oh, I will, I will."

Bertram leaned back in his chair and stared up at the cracks on his ceiling. "The day Bertram Cummings renounces his nerdship, once and for all!"

11

As Louise walked into the auditorium, it occurred to her that this was her very first student council meeting. There had been no such thing as student council in grade school or junior high. She'd never even heard of it till she'd come to Masters. When someone had once explained to her what it was and what the council did, and how things were voted on, and how you got elected, it all sounded a little silly. After all, the whole thing was really controlled by seniors, and the seniors were really controlled by teachers, and the teachers were really controlled by Mrs. Mead, and Mrs. Mead controlled everything anyway, so what was the point? The only thing they really had any control over was what to do with their money, which they'd made from dances or car washes, or bake sales. And usually, Louise knew, they argued for weeks, voted, and decided they'd spend the money on more dances, car washes, and bake sales.

Personally, Louise knew she'd rather spend her homerooms reading in the library.

"Hey!" someone shouted from across the room.

Louise turned and saw Mike, Chuck, and Dennis standing in an alcove behind the council table.

"Hi," Louise said, as she walked up to them.

"Where's Bertram?" Mike snapped.

"How should I know?"

"You called him and he said he was gonna be here."

Dennis chimed, "That's right, he said—"

Louise cut in, "He's probably getting the AV equipment."

Mike shook his head. "It's all in there," he said, pointing to a blue door a few feet away, "and it's locked. And the meeting starts in three minutes."

"Well," Louise said, "all I know is, he said he'd be here." She checked her watch.

"He'd better be," Mike said.

"He'd better," Chuck said.

"Yeah," Dennis said.

They waited, watching the people trickle in in groups of two, four, six, all talking excitedly among themselves. Word had gotten out yesterday that this meeting was going to be different, that something was going to be presented, something special. A surprise.

The auditorium began to fill up. Soon there were no seats and people were standing at the back.

Louise heard bits of conversation:

"I don't know, what have you heard?"

"Just that it's something weird . . ."

". . . something freshman weird."

"If it's freshman, then it's definitely weird . . ."

". . . I heard it was—"

"—yeah, me too—"

"—and that Mrs. Mead—"

"—I heard the same thing—"

"—and—"

"—right, right—"

From a door at the back of the room the council president, Steve Warren, entered, followed by four council members.

"Great," Mike moaned. "Now the meeting's gonna start, and where the hell is—?"

Louise saw him. He was hurrying through the double doors, blinking behind those big, black-rimmed glasses.

She waved her arm, shouting over the din, "Bertram! Hey! Over here!"

He craned his neck to see, waved, and pushed his way past a dozen bodies. When he finally came up to Louise, he was breathing hard.

"Sorry." He took a big breath. "Sorry I'm . . . late."

Mike, Chuck, and Dennis said nothing. Louise had told them the night before that the best thing would be if she talked to Bertram and they kept their mouths shut.

"Do you have the key to the AV room?" Louise asked.

"Uh, yeah, I do. It's—" He reached into the front pocket of his pants and felt around. "I think I put them —" He fumbled around, then tried the other pocket. As he was doing this, his books slipped and splattered against the floor. "Ooops, um, wait a sec—" He reached into his back pockets.

Mike rolled his eyes, and Louise could tell he was about to say something. She threw a deadly look at him. He closed his mouth.

"Ah!" Bertram said, as he reached into his shirt pocket and produced a ring of keys.

Steve Warren and his fellow council members had seated themselves at the table and were now ready to start. Warren picked up the gavel and pounded it twice. The room grew a little quieter. He pounded again.

Bertram picked one of the keys on the ring and tried to get it into the lock. It wouldn't go. "Jeez, I thought it was that one," he mumbled, then tried another. Louise noticed there were ten keys on the ring.

"Order!" Steve Warren shouted, as he pounded. "Order!"

Bertram continued to try keys, none of which fit. "Maybe this is the wrong set of keys," he said, half to himself.

Louise looked at Mike. His face was bright red and going purple.

Bertram tried still another key. He shook his head.

Louise said, "Let me take a look." Bertram handed her the ring. She examined it and picked a key. "Try this one."

He did. It worked. Bertram grinned. "How'd you know?" he asked.

"It had AV ROOM written on it," she said.

They went in. Bertram switched on a light.

Outside, in the aud, things had begun to quiet down a little. "Okay, that's better," Steve Warren was saying.

In the AV Room, Bertram waded through the tables and shelves, projectors, record players, radios, and television sets. He disappeared around the corner. They waited.

"I hate him so much," Mike said quietly.

"Shhhhh!" from Louise.

"The video screen, right?" Bertram said.

"Right," Louise said.

A pause; silence. Then the sound of something crashing down, a "Woops" from Bertram.

"Are you okay, Bertram?" Louise asked.

"Fine, fine," he said, wheeling the big screen and TV projector out. "Where do you want this?"

"Let's bring it out next to the council desk," she said. She helped Bertram get it through the door and set it where everyone could see it.

Steve Warren banged his gavel one last time, then laid it down. "Now, we've got a bunch of stuff to get through today, so let's read the agenda and get started." The vice-president, Monica Favers, picked up a sheet of paper and began to read.

As Louise and Bertram were straightening out the screen, Louise saw Mrs. Mead slip in and take a seat with a few teachers at the back of the room.

Bertram whispered to Louise, "Okay, I've got it focused and everything. You want it set at any particular channel?"

Louise shook her head. "How do I turn it on?"

Bertram pointed. "This button here. Anytime you're ready."

"Okay, thanks a lot Bertram, I really appre—"

She was cut off by Monica Favers, who stood and said, "But first, we have several people from the . . . freshman class who have a video presentation. And here to tell us about it is Michael Grodey."

"Godey," Mike corrected, as he stepped up to the desk.

Monica shrugged and sat down.

"Godey," Mike said to the audience, then cleared his throat loudly. He continued, "Now, everybody, we've got something very, very important to show you. What we have here is the most . . . important, most . . . amazing thing that has ever happened in the . . ."

As Mike spoke, droning on, getting off the track, and generally boring everyone to death, Bertram slipped away from the video screen and found himself an empty seat. Looking over his shoulder, he located Dalton standing near the doors, his book bag slung over his shoulder. Bertram waved. Dalton waved back half-heartedly.

"I know that's saying a lot," Mike was saying, "but really, it's not enough at all—at least, that's what you're gonna say, once you see this, because it's what I said—I mean, I really couldn't believe . . ."

An older girl next to Bertram whispered to her friend, "What *is* he talking about?" The friend shrugged.

"And you should all just keep one thing in mind, too," Mike went on, "that we—that's Chuck and Dennis and Louise and me—we were the first ones to be contacted. Okay? . . . Okay, well, that's just about it."

"Good," somebody in the audience said, and a couple of people around him laughed.

Steve Warren banged his gavel. They quieted down.

"Okay," Mike said, nodding. "Chuck, turn on the set."

Chuck looked at it. "I—I don't know how, Mike."

Some people in the front row who heard the exchange laughed and shook their heads. Even Steve Warren laughed.

Now's the time, Bertram thought to himself, and reached down and pulled up his pant leg. Strapped to his leg with duct tape was the remote control unit he'd put together last night; it could activate the broadcast unit automatically. A video tape of Bertram in the alien outfit would be inserted into a VCR hooked up to the machine. The tape would be broadcast as if it were happening live.

"I can do it," Louise said, rolling her eyes and stepping between Chuck and Mike. She kneeled down, hit the button, and stood back.

Mike looked at his watch.

The screen, which was actually just a large piece of curved nylon, flickered as the TV image was projected into it. It was big enough so everybody in the room could see what it was: a dishwasher commercial.

Bertram struggled with the duct tape, fought to get the little black box out. He started to sweat at the temples. He pulled and jerked and felt around for a loose edge, but the tape was too strong. . . .

The dishwasher commercial continued, uninterrupted. People began to rustle in their seats. Somebody coughed.

Bertram reached down with both hands and pulled his ankle up where he could see it. He yanked at the tape with both hands. He picked at it with his nail until an edge came up, then he pulled and unwound it.

The older girl next to him gave him an annoyed glance.

The audience was getting really restless now. The dishwasher commercial had ended and there was a game show on.

"Hey," somebody yelled, "the freshmen have discovered TV."

Everybody laughed. Steve Warren started banging his gavel.

Bertram pulled the remote control unit out of the sticky-tape goo, wiped it off on his pant leg, and hit the BROADCAST button. At that moment, he knew, the whole system would whirr to life in his room—the buttons would light, the computer screen would lock and verify the coordinates, the dish antenna would turn itself and begin radiating its interruptive signal, and finally the tape would drop into the video machine and . . .

"Order!" Steve Warren shouted. "Order. . . . OR-DER!" Nobody paid any attention, so Steve stood up, lifted his gavel as high as he could, and brought it down with a furious, explosive *bang*. And followed this with a bellowing "ORRRRDERRRRRR!"

But he was screaming in a room that was totally silent, to an audience staring intently at a screen that had suddenly changed. A housewife winning a roomful of furniture had been replaced by a bald, green, large-eyed alien waving thumbless hands and, in a warbling extraterrestrial voice, saying "Gr-eet-ings."

Silence in the big room. Shocked silence, perhaps even disbelieving silence, but silence nonetheless.

Steve Warren looked at the screen and dropped his gavel. It hit the floor with a pitiful bang, then broke in half.

The alien on the screen tilted its head and said, "I am Non of Zenka."

Bertram watched, as transfixed as everyone else. But he felt distant, uninvolved. Watching himself on the screen made him feel as if he weren't in the room at all, but watching from behind some two-way mirror in the wall, waiting for everyone's reaction to the final scene in a play he'd constructed. And in some ways it *was* like a play, because like a play it meant nothing without the audience.

The alien on the screen said (as Bertram knew he would), "I have contacted you through these young ones to tell you something of great importance."

Bertram glanced at Mike, Chuck, Dennis, and Louise. They were huddled together in the corner, watching, smiling, loving every minute.

"But," the alien continued, "in order for me to tell you this thing, you must first believe in me and who I am."

The older girl next to Bertram said to her friend, "Is this some kind of joke?" Her friend shrugged, not taking her eyes off the screen for a second.

The alien paused, looked out as if he were surveying the group of people, actually seeing them. "We have some unbelievers among you. . . . Hmmmmmmmm. . . . Interesting." He paused before going on. "How encouraging that is to know, that not everyone here is as easily fooled as these four."

The smiles on the faces of Louise, Mike, Chuck, and Dennis froze for a moment, then vanished.

"It's really sort of dangerous, if you think about it," the alien went on, the warble in his voice becoming less pronounced, "how anyone with a camera, some broadcast equipment, and a tape deck can manufacture—a man from another planet." On the words "another planet" the electronic alien voice disappeared completely and Bertram's own voice could be heard clearly. A few people in the audience buzzed and whispered. Bertram the Alien went on, "How anyone with these things could fool a group of . . . average intelligence into believing just about anything."

A no-thumb hand reached up, grasped the head, and with very little fuss, popped the head off and set it down. Bertram's slightly sweaty, bigger-than-life face beamed out at everyone. There was a single, collective gasp, then a few chuckles.

Sitting in his seat and watching, Bertram wished he'd

been able to comb his hair after taking off the alien head. He looked awful.

"Fortunately," Bertram on screen said, "my message wasn't a dangerous one, but it could have been. And who knows what people will do? Especially when all they care about is getting their names in the paper." The image of Bertram shrugged. "Anyway, sorry to take up your time. Hope you didn't mind."

Everyone applauded as the image faded and the game show came back on. Then the older girl sitting next to Bertram looked at him, looked away, looked back, and shouted, "Hey! You're him!" She stood up and pointed. "Here he is! Hey, you guys . . . !"

Bertram stood up as a mob of people rushed at him, all holding out their hands, slapping him on the back, ruffling his hair, saying "Good going, Bertram." "Good job." "Great stuff." "Wow." "Yeah." "Excellent sting." "Really got 'em." "Good enough." "Loved it." "Loved it." "Loved it."

Bertram just grinned and drank it all up like a desert rat at an oasis. The most popular people at school—the captain of the football team, Ray Barry, the head cheerleader, Lillian Moss, the editor of the paper, Mitch Sheen—swarmed around him to congratulate him; all the older kids he'd dreamed of meeting and talking to, the giants who roamed the halls of the school, were asking to talk to *him*, saying things like "Hey, guy, why don't you sit at my table at lunch tomorrow?" and "Why don't we get together after school?"

Hands he'd dreamed of shaking were all being thrust at him, and he fought to grasp each one, to look into each person's eyes, to savor every moment.

But pretty soon Steve Warren was banging the table with the palm of his hand, calling for order. "Okay, you guys, come on, we've got stuff to do. . . . Yeah, okay, the fun's over, now either stay for the meeting, or clear out."

Bertram pulled himself away from a couple of people when he saw Mrs. Mead pass in front of him. She either didn't see him or didn't feel like dealing with him now. In any case, she went right past him and swooped down on the four in the corner: Mike, Louise, Chuck, and Dennis, all looking as if they'd been hit in the head with a safe.

Bertram strained to hear what Mrs. Mead was saying to them, as she shook an angry finger at each.

"And I want all of you in my office today after school."

"But Mrs. Mead—" Mike pleaded.

"In my office after school, all of you!" she shouted, and Mike backed down. "We had an agreement, remember? A promise? Well, we're going to discuss the terms of that promise."

With that, she turned and walked toward the double doors. She passed Bertram again, and this time looked him in the eye. The look was not overwhelmingly kind, but not nearly as harsh as the one she'd given the four.

The majority of the people in the auditorium started for the doors. But they continued to swarm around Bertram, even after Dalton had joined up with him and they'd started to walk down the hall together.

"Great, Bertram." "Fantastic." "Where'd you ever get the idea?" "Absolutely awesome." "Those four— what a buncha jerks."

"You did it, Bertram," Dalton said. "I have to admit— you pulled it off."

Bertram smiled and shrugged. But it was hard to be

humble when surrounded by two dozen admirers. I guess this is how it feels to be a rock star, he thought.

As he and the group surrounding him started to round the corner leading to the main hall, they felt someone trying to push through, someone in a hurry. A few people stepped aside. Bertram felt whoever it was elbow past, then saw a blond head streak by and plow past the people in her way.

"Hey, it's that girl," somebody said.

"Who?"

"You know, Louise What's-her-name."

Bertram looked through the opening Louise had made in the crowd. She was running down the hall, toward the library.

"Hey," somebody said, "she was cryin'."

Somebody else laughed. "Wouldn't *you* be?"

"I guess so."

Bertram suddenly felt tired, as if all the energy he'd been pumped full of in the last few minutes had been siphoned out of him. He suddenly wanted to go somewhere and be alone, think things over, talk to Dalton.

"Hey, Bertram . . ."

"Hey."

"Hey, tell us how you did it . . ."

"How'd you make that mask?"

"And the voice?"

"Hey, come on, Bertram, how'd you do it?"

"Yeah, and how come?"

"Yeah, what'd you do it for, Bertram?"

"Bertram?"

12

It was a bitterly cold morning. Dalton's gloved fingers gripped the zipper of his jacket and tugged, trying to get it up just a little higher. Since he hadn't been able to find his scarf that morning, and since all the other scarves in the house had been taken, he was left with an exposed neck and a zipper that wouldn't go all the way up.

"Hey, Dalton!" Bertram yelled, shuffling clumsily up the icy sidewalk. Dalton stopped to wait. Every few steps Bertram took he slipped a bit, nearly lost his balance, then by some miracle managed to right himself.

"Hey, Bertram," Dalton said.

"Jeez, some morning, huh?"

"Yeah."

They walked in silence for a few minutes. As they neared the school, they began walking past clumps of people huddled against the cold, talking, waiting for the first bell to ring. Some were reading the school paper, which had just come out.

Dalton and Bertram continued to walk in silence.

"Hi, Bertie!" A beautiful girl smiled and waved at Bertram.

"Hi," Bertram said nonchalantly.

Dalton looked at Bertram. Bertram looked straight ahead, saying nothing. A small, almost unnoticeable smile played at the edges of his mouth.

"Hi, Bertram," a big jocky guy said. He slapped Bertram on the shoulder as he walked past.

"Hiya," Bertram said. When the guy was well out of sight, he rubbed his shoulder.

Another beautiful girl happened past. "Great picture, Bertram," she said.

Bertram shrugged, nodded.

"Picture?" Dalton asked.

"All right, Bertram!" a guy shouted from a passing Corvette.

Bertram waved. "Get outta here, you crazy nuts!" And he laughed casually.

"What picture?" Dalton asked.

"I think it's right here," Bertram replied, steering them over to a tight clump of people, all bending over something. When they got closer, Dalton could see they were grabbing copies of the school paper, and as they pushed through the people to get their copies, several people around them said, "It's Bertram!" "Hey, Bertram, how's it going?" "Great picture, Bertram!" Bertram just smiled politely as all this went on, shook a few hands, nodded, said nothing. When he and Dalton had gotten their papers, they walked on.

Ah-hah, Dalton thought, as he unfolded it to the front page. On it was a banner headline: STUDENT COUNCIL MEETING INTERRUPTED BY 'ALIEN.' And below that an enormous picture of Bertram. It was actually a blowup of his eighth-grade class picture, and it was not a great picture. First of all, his hair was a twisted tangle, the result of having walked under an active air vent just before the picture was snapped. (Dalton knew this because he'd been standing in line behind Bertram, waiting for *his* picture to be taken.) Second of all, he'd dropped his glasses and broken them that morning, so in the picture they were taped together at the bridge, which caused them to tilt slightly to the left. And third of all, he did not react well to the flashbulb when it went off, so behind those taped, tilting glasses his eyes formed two molelike slits.

"This picture isn't as bad as I remember," Bertram said.

Dalton just nodded and said nothing. He scanned the article, which began:

> At yesterday's Student Council meeting, which was packed with observers who'd been told something "special" and "different" would be happening, four members of the freshman class, Dennis Kutchinson, Charles Benson, Louise Baker, and Michael Grodey told all present that they had something "never before seen" to show everyone. Grodey went on to say it was the "most important, most amazing thing that has ever happened" and that he and his three cohorts were "the first to be contacted."

Dalton skipped the part describing the alien and everyone's reaction, and scanned the last few paragraphs:

> The "alien" that the four believed had contacted them from the Andromeda galaxy was in fact the brainchild of freshman Bertram

Cummings. The hoax was perpetrated, Cummings explained, through the use of a "TV channel interceptor" which he had been working on as a science project. Cummings went on to say that the purpose of the hoax had been to show everyone the danger of "believing everything you see."

"People have a tendency to accept whatever's put in front of them," Cummings said in a later interview. "Especially anything that comes from television, and talks directly to them. Something like the TV channel interceptor in the wrong hands could really mess up people's minds, unless we all learn to be a little more pragmatic."

"Pragmatic?" Dalton asked. "What's that mean?"
"Logical," Bertram answered. "Scientific."
"Oh."
The last sentence of the article read:

Cummings said he bore no ill will to the four victims of the hoax, and that they were chosen solely because of their overwhelming belief in life on other worlds.

Dalton shook his head after reading that part, folded the paper, and stuck it under his arm. "You know what happens to people who lie, don't you?"

"Yeah, they're damned to a life of eternal gym class."

"Well, I've got to admit, right on down the line, it worked. It's amazing, but it worked. You didn't get in trouble at all?"

"Mrs. Mead talked to me for a few minutes after

school and gave me the old 'If this ever happens again' thing."

"What about Mike and those guys?"

Bertram grinned. "Detention. Every day after school for three weeks."

"And Louise?"

Bertram didn't stop grinning, but Dalton noticed his eyes go funny, and it took him a few seconds to answer. "Same thing, I guess."

"You really did it."

"I really did."

"Revenge is sweet."

"It sure is."

They walked through the front doors of the school, into the main hall, and joined the flow of people heading for their lockers.

"Hi, Bertram."

"Hiya, Bertram."

"Hey, Bertie."

"How's it goin', Bert?"

They rounded a corner. The first bell rang.

"Well," Bertram said, "I better get to class."

"Okay," Dalton said. "See you in the library at homeroom?"

"See you there." He nodded and walked toward his locker. As he did, Dalton watched heads turn, people call out, then say to each other, "That's him, that's the guy who did the—you know—the thing."

Dalton took the paper out from under his arm, unfolded it, and looked at the lopsided, squinting face of his best friend. Fame is a curious thing, he thought, a curious thing indeed.

Bertram strode out of the locker room feeling refreshed and invigorated. It was the first time in his life he could remember feeling that way after gym class. True, the sport they had played was team badminton, and true, that wasn't exactly a grueling Olympic sport. But today Bertram felt full of confidence as he slipped into his shorts and T-shirt; felt fit and energetic as he took the badminton racquet into his hand and marched onto the court with the others. He'd felt blazing energy as the birdie came his way and he spun for a backhand, swung, and knocked the thing over the net. Time after time he was able to hold his section of the court, and even managed to weather the embarrassment of planting a misswung forehand into Alice Denker's kneecap. Afterwards, several of his teammates slapped him on the back and congratulated him on a good game, and even Mr. Donovan nodded in his direction and gave an encouraging wink.

So after a hot, soapy shower, some good locker room talk ("I hit Alice on purpose," he lied, "so I could watch her bend over") and a splash of Brut aftershave (borrowed from Alex Feldman, one locker down) how could he *help* but feel refreshed and invigorated?

As he walked down the hall toward the library, smiles and waves continued to come his way.

"Bertram, what's up?"

"Hey, Bert, let's get together."

"Hey, B, awesome picture."

"Hiya, Bertram."

"Good to see you, Bertram."

It was sort of a relief to get into the library with Dalton and sit at a table in a far corner where no one would bother them.

"Hiding from your fans?" Dalton asked.

"I just need a rest from smiling."

"Being a superstar's not easy."

"Yeah, I know, it's a tough job, but somebody's gotta do it."

Something caught Dalton's eye; he looked over his shoulder and said, "You really want a rest from smiling?"

"What are you talking about?"

Dalton shifted in his seat and pointed. "Why don't you go ask what she's doing after school?"

Louise had just walked in and sat herself in her usual place on the couch.

"What are you saying? You think she's mad at me?"

"Oh, *no*. Why on earth would she be mad at *you?*"

"Well, why should she? We're even now."

"Okay," Dalton said. "If you're even, go shake hands, tell her there's no hard feelings."

Bertram rolled his eyes. "I don't have to prove anything."

"Who's asking you to prove anything?"

"You are."

"No, I'm not."

"Yes, you are."

"Going and shaking hands with her won't prove anything to me. I *know* she hates your guts."

"She does not." Bertram sat back and folded his arms, then unfolded them and drummed the table with his fingers. "Does she?"

"Go see."

Bertram just sat. There was no reason why it should be hard for him to go up and say hi, make some chat, then go sit back down. After all, everything was out in the open now. It wasn't like before, when he didn't know if she knew he was even alive. He was famous now. Everybody knew who he was. Even gym class had gotten better. And besides, Louise wasn't the type to hold a grudge over something stupid, something as trivial as a three-week detention, especially after what *she* did to *him*. If she was mature—and he knew she was— she would realize that what he did was . . . normal, and would forgive him, just as he had forgiven her now.

Bertram stood up.

"That's the stuff," Dalton said.

"It's silly to sit and pretend we don't know each other."

"Of course. You're both adults."

"That's right."

"Mature, able to get over things."

"Absolutely."

"Besides, she's a girl—how hard could she hit you?"

"Ha-ha." Bertram straightened the cuffs of his shirt, stepped around the table, and walked over to the couch. Louise was immersed in another dance magazine, so it was a few seconds before she sensed someone hovering over her.

She didn't look up.

Bertram cleared his throat, then said, "Hey, Louise."

She still wouldn't look up. She turned a page in her magazine.

Bertram began to sense that this wasn't such a good idea. "Uh, Louise?" he said, a little more softly.

Another magazine page was flipped.

"Louise, listen—"

She looked up now, and the coldness of her expression, the sheer hatred shining out of her eyes, startled Bertram and caused him to gasp. A tiny air bubble began to form in his throat. For a moment he was unable to breathe or speak.

Louise, meanwhile, turned, picked up her dance bag, and stuffed the magazine inside.

Bertram opened his mouth, fighting for breath, but the bubble of air was now creeping down his throat into his chest; it felt as if he were swallowing a ball bearing. He thumped his chest with his fist.

Louise looked at him as she stood to leave.

He thumped his chest again, felt the bubble drop somewhere into his stomach, and took a much needed breath. Louise was heading for the door now. He took a couple of quick steps after her.

"Louise," he said quickly, "I—*hic*—I—*hic*—I—*hic, hic, hic*—!" He coughed, thumped his chest again, then realized what had happened. He'd given himself the hiccups.

It was too late.

Louise had walked furiously out of the library without listening to a single word he had tried to say.

Dalton came up behind him, and clapped a hand on his shoulder.

"Looks like you were right again," he said. "I can't see that she's holding a grudge."

"Hic," said Bertram.

"And that new smooth attitude you've adopted—"

"Hic."

"Really does the trick. Just a matter of time and she's all yours."

"She's really mad I think."

"No, she's just playing hard to get."

"No, I—*hic*—"

"You want a drink of water?"

"No, *hic*—I'll be fine as soon as I get my—*hic*—breath."

"Well, what are you gonna do?"

Bertram shrugged. "What can I do—*hic?*" He cleared his throat and thumped his chest. "The girl scares me."

Dalton and Bertram walked back to their table and sat down. The first thing to do was get rid of the hiccups. Dalton said his mother's method of doing that was to breathe into a paper bag for a few minutes. So Dalton emptied all the stuff out of his lunch bag, then had Bertram put the open end of the bag around his nose and mouth, hold it tight, and take deep breaths.

Bertram's hiccuping stopped for a few moments as he breathed in and out, and the brown paper bag filled, then deflated, filled, then deflated.

"How's that?" Dalton asked.

"Bag smells like onions," Bertram said.

"Don't worry. It's good for you."

"I *hate* onions."

"I do too. Except on peanut butter sandwiches."

"Uuuchhhh, I'm gonna throw up."

"Well, do it in your own bag. . . . And keep breathing."

Bertram breathed in silence.

"I feel dizzy," he said after a few minutes.

"It's just hyperventilation."

"No, it's these *onions.*"

"Stop exaggerating. How do you feel?"

"Like a grilled cheeseburger." He took the bag off his face, handed it back to Dalton, and inhaled a few deep breaths of fresh air.

"Better?" Dalton asked.

Bertram nodded.

"Works every time." He put his lunch back into the bag.

"So what am I gonna do about Louise?"

"Well, what do you want to do about Louise?"

"Well, I don't want her to hate me . . . I don't want anybody to hate me."

"I wouldn't say Mike and friends were overly fond of you."

"Put it this way—I don't want anything human to hate me."

"Ah." Dalton nodded.

A decision was reached about Louise.

And the decision was: flowers.

Dalton's reasoning was, flowers told a girl that you were willing to make an effort, that you'd gone out, spent not-a-small-sum, and here you were, putting yourself on the line. Flowers were the thing for apologizing.

"So where do you get flowers?" Bertram asked.

"At a flower shop."

"We couldn't just slip into somebody's yard and pick some?"

"Yeah, roots and all, covered in dirt, and wrapped in wax paper. You're the last of the great romantics, Bertram."

There was a flower shop just a few blocks from school, right next to the R and R drug store. If Bertram were careful he could slip out one of the side doors of the school, get the flowers, be back just before science class started, and give them to Louise at her locker.

So Bertram did just that. Dalton distracted one of the hall monitors near the door, and Bertram was able to scurry past and out without being seen. Just before going into the shop, Bertram checked on his financial situation: two dollars and seventy-five cents and two air mail stamps.

He walked into the shop, glanced at the lady behind the counter, then started to browse. He was shocked by the prices. Tiny little potted plants were seven, eight, nine dollars. Roses were a dollar fifty *a piece.* Most bouquets were over five dollars.

Bertram asked the lady behind the counter, who smelled more like a flower than any flower he'd ever gotten a whiff of, what he could get for two dollars and seventy-five cents. Except for single flowers, she told him, there wasn't much. She then added that for three dollars she had some "slightly wilted" bouquets in the back.

Bertram asked her if she would accept air mail stamps as currency.

She looked at him a moment over the half-glasses sitting on the end of her nose, smiled, and said that in this case she would.

So Bertram left the shop holding a bouquet of pale, wrinkled violets and drooping baby's breath. But what the heck, nobody could say they weren't flowers.

"Okay," Bertram said, peering around the corner, "here she comes."

"Good luck," Dalton said, moving off.

"Right, right."

A swarm of people came tramping into the locker area; several waved and said hello to Bertram. Bertram nodded back cordially. He leaned against the wall and waited, the bouquet clutched tight in his fist, his palms sweating all over the dry, green stems.

Louise and a friend came into sight. Louise was walking fast enough so that she didn't see Bertram as she came around the corner. Bertram stepped up behind her.

"Um, Louise," he said, but his voice was drowned out by the hall noise, so she continued walking.

"Louise," he said again, practically shouting this time. Louise jumped, then whirled around. The same hard eyes drilled into Bertram.

"What?" she snapped.

"Ummm," he said, holding the flowers out. "Errrrr . . ."

Louise looked at the flowers, then at Bertram. Her face seemed to soften for a moment; the eyes seemed to warm a bit.

Bertram said, "I just picked these up. I just wanted to say that . . . that . . . uh . . ." Why the hell was it he could never put a sentence together around her?

"Bertram," Louise said. "I don't understand why you did what you did to me. I mean, I guess I can figure out why you wanted to get back at Mike and those guys, but I always liked you . . . and—and what you did was so mean. . . ." She blinked quickly and her voice quavered on the last few words.

But something in Bertram suddenly flared. What was this crying bit, anyway? Like she was some innocent victim or something.

"All I did," he said, his voice suddenly sharpening with anger, "was get back at you—"

"Get back at me for what?"

"For—for . . . you know . . ."

"No, I don't."

"For that letter you wrote."

"What letter?"

"The letter!"

"I don't know what letter you're talking about!"

"The letter you left in my locker."

Louise shook her head. Bertram looked closely into her eyes.

He went on, "The one that said how you'd always been wanting to . . . to meet me and—"

"I never wrote you any letter like that!"

"Well then you let Mike and those guys do it!"

"I didn't let Mike and those guys do anything!"

The second class bell rang. The few students still at their lockers slammed them shut and ran.

Louise and Bertram didn't budge.

"You didn't, huh?" Bertram said.

"No, I didn't."

"But you laughed at me, Louise!"

"But you acted like such a jerk!"

"But . . ." Bertram breathed heavily, fought to find another accusation to hurl. Slowly, however, it was beginning to dawn on him that he had no accusations to hurl, that somewhere along the line things had become just a bit confused.

"But," he said again.

"Look, Bertram, I really have to get to class."

"I do too," Bertram said. "We have the same class, remember?"

"Well, I'm not just gonna stand here and fight about this all day. I don't know what we're fighting about."

"Me either."

"Besides, I'm not talking to you."

She turned and started to walk to Barnes's class.

"Do you want the flowers?" he asked.

She stopped walking but didn't turn and didn't look back. "No," she said.

"Well, why not?"

"Because I am mad at you and I want you to leave me alone." Louise started to walk again.

A few steps later, Bertram called, "Well, do you want to talk about this?"

She stopped again.

"I could take you someplace . . . after school. Get a Coke maybe."

Louise said, "Even if I *was* talking to you, I couldn't."

"Why?"

"I've got detention." She turned and walked out of sight.

Bertram dumped the flowers in a garbage can and buried them under all the papers and milk cartons. Then he went to science class, dreading it.

When he walked in, he caught five very cold stares: Louise's, Dennis's, Chuck's, Mike's. And Mr. Barnes's.

Louise's stare he had naturally expected. Same with the Unholy Trio's, though he knew that his battle with Mike was finally over. Mike would never bother him again. Never talk back. Never trip him in the library or call him a nerd to his face. Too much had changed and oddly, Bertram felt himself feeling a little sad as he settled onto his stool. He realized that he had taken away Mike's only true weapon: his image of himself. Stripped of that, he was just another kid among hundreds; tolerated but never well liked.

But it was Barnes's stare that sent a small chill down Bertram's spine. And, when at the end of class, Barnes said, "Bertram, I'd like to see you a moment," he felt his throat go dry, because he knew what Barnes wanted.

He wanted Bertram to defend his scientific ethics, something Bertram knew he would not be able to do. So it was left to Barnes to do the talking. What he said to Bertram was short, to the point, and stung like hell.

He said: "I expected a lot more from you."

13

Dalton found Bertram in a far corner of the cafeteria, staring into space, his feet propped up on the empty table in front of him, his head tilted back.

It was the lunch hour. The cafeteria was just starting to fill up. A line was forming for food. People were dropping quarters into the vending machines, getting milk, soda, candy, chips.

But Bertram was just sitting. Staring.

"Hey," Dalton said, "wanna bite of this great peanut butter and onion sandwich?"

Bertram let his head bob forward. "Are you trying to make me sick again?"

"I guess it didn't go so good with Louise."

He shook his head. "Not so good."

Dalton unwrapped his lunch, started to eat. "Flowers didn't help?"

"I would've done just as well with a bowling ball."

"Well," Dalton said, biting into his sandwich (which, by the way, was not really peanut butter and onion), "anything worth having is worth working for."

"That's incredibly profound."

"What do you want? I'm just a freshman in high school."

Bertram shook his head, leaned forward, and set his chin on his folded arms. He sighed.

"This is amazing," Dalton said.

"What?"

"What I'm watching here."

"What are you talking about?"

"You are acting exactly the same way you were a month ago. A month ago when all you did was complain about how unpopular you were. How you couldn't get Louise to notice you. How you were terrible in gym. How Godey and his friends were making your life miserable."

Three of the school's cheerleaders walked by. They smiled at Bertram.

"Hi, Bertram."

"Hi, Bertram."

"Hi, Bertram, hee-hee."

Bertram waved back. "Hi, girls."

"Now," Dalton said, "cheerleaders say hello to you in the cafeteria. Will nothing make you happy?"

"Dalton, Louise had nothing to do with that thing Mike and his friends pulled. She just told me. She didn't know about it at all."

"So?"

" 'So?' So, I got back at her for no reason. I put her through that humiliation for nothing. She has a three-week detention. People laugh at her all the time."

"Look at the bright side, will you?"

"Bright side?"

"She knows who you are. And you know she knows who you are."

"It doesn't make any difference. I'm around her, I try and talk to her, I still can't put two words together. I mean, it's like I know all the things I want to say, I can even think of how I want to say them, but nothing ever comes out right. And it's like I don't even have a chance, really. Before, she used to just look at me like I was the town idiot, now she looks at me like the town hangman. It's a totally no-win situation."

"No situation is a no-win situation."

"How is this situation a win situation?"

"If I told you everything, life would lose its mystery. There'd be no fun, no discovery."

"You're really hilarious today."

"I guarantee you—go home, think this thing over. You'll figure a way to crack this thing."

Bertram shook his head. "No way."

"You don't see it, do you?"

"I guess I don't."

"All you want to do is really break the ice with her, right? Just have one shot at telling her how you really feel—that this whole thing was a mix-up, that you're really sorry, that you're ready to take the wedding vows right now—"

Bertram rolled his eyes and sat back. "God, you're a pain sometimes."

"Okay, maybe that's going a little too far. But you know what you want to say. You just have to find a *way to say it*. Hint, hint."

Bertram looked at his friend blankly.

"You know—communication. Hint, hint."

He still didn't get it.

"*Vis*ual communication, as in *vision,* as in *tele*port, as in *tele*—"

Bertram sat up as if a pin had been thrust into his butt. He snapped his fingers. "That's it!"

"I knew you'd get it eventually." He looked at his sandwich. "Last bite—going, going, gone." He popped it into his mouth.

"You're disgusting, you know, but you're a lot smarter than you look."

Dalton swallowed and said, "A lot."

Mrs. Baker was sitting in front of the television set in the living room. The evening news was on. She was ironing some freshly done laundry. Her husband walked into the room and crossed over to the set. As he bent down to adjust the color, the picture suddenly jumped, the sound crackled, and a fourteen-year-old boy with brown hair and thick eyeglasses stared out at the Bakers and said; "Um, hi. I'm really sorry to bother you, but if Louise is there, I'd like to talk to her."

Mr. Baker straightened up and looked at his wife.

Mrs. Baker started ironing the sleeve of a blouse and called: "Louise, television again!"

Mr. Baker sighed and shook his head. "That's *twice* he's interrupted the news."

Louise came bounding down the stairs. She walked into the room, looked, and saw Bertram.

Bertram said, "Louise? This is Bertram. If you're there, please don't turn me off—" As he said this, the picture jiggled and the Bakers were suddenly looking at Bertram's feet. "Uh, hang on a sec—gotta fix this tripod." The picture jumped some more as Bertram fiddled with the camera.

Louise sat down and looked at him. She had to laugh. The TV picture finally straightened out. Bertram spent a second refocusing, then sat back down on his stool and looked out at them again.

"There," he said. "Louise, I'll make this quick, and I promise this is the last time I'll ever be on your TV. I don't really get a big kick out of interrupting people's TV shows. All I wanted was the chance to tell you how sorry I am. I can't seem to say it when I'm around you. I get all tongue-tied . . . When I'm around you sometimes, I couldn't get a noun and verb together to save my life." He laughed nervously. "But seriously, I'd like to start over with you. No more outfits, no more flowers, no more aliens. Just what you see here . . . Anyway, I hope you're home to hear this. And I hope . . . we can get to be friends."

Louise got up and reached for the phone.

"So," Bertram-on-screen said, "this is station B-E-R-T signing off, wishing you and yours a happy and safe—"

A phone in Bertram's room rang.

Bertram said, "Hang on, I've got to get the phone." He walked offscreen, and at the same time Louise heard him say "Hello?" into her ear, she heard "Hello?" come out of the TV. Quite a neat trick, she thought to herself, as she said "Bertram? This is Louise."

"Louise?" the two voices of Bertram said.

"Hi."

There was a pause. Louise looked at her set. Bertram stepped back in front of the camera, smiled brightly, and flipped a button. The evening news was back on.

"So," Bertram said into the phone. "Funny you should call. What's on your mind?"

Louise didn't answer, just smiled and shook her head.

About the Author

John McNamara is originally from Grand Rapids, Michigan. He is the author of the play *Present Tense*, which won the 1982 Young Playwrights' Festival and was produced at the Circle Repertory Company in New York, and the original television script for *Revenge of the Nerd*. Currently, he is working on several other plays and *The Jacqueline Week*, a novel.

He claims never to have been a nerd.